The back door was open and there was no sign of Rachel.

Jacob hurried over to see her tossing a bag of garbage up and into the dumpster.

Out of nowhere, a white vehicle pulled up and a man jumped out from the back seat. He threw a hood over Rachel's head and jerked her toward the car.

"No! Stop!" Jacob lunged forward, grabbing the edge of the door before the guy could close it. Then he grabbed on to Rachel's arm. "Let her go!"

The man inside abruptly shoved Rachel toward him as the driver hit the gas. Jacob managed to pull Rachel out of harm's way seconds before the vehicle peeled away through the alley.

He clutched her against him, his heart thudding painfully against his ribs as he realized how close Rachel had come to being kidnapped.

Laura Scott has always loved romance and read faith-based books by Grace Livingston Hill in her teenage years. She's thrilled to have been given the opportunity to retire from thirty-eight years of nursing to become a full-time author. Laura has published over thirty books for Love Inspired Suspense. She has two adult children and lives in Milwaukee, Wisconsin, with her husband of thirty-five years. Please visit Laura at laurascottbooks.com, as she loves to hear from her readers.

Books by Laura Scott

Love Inspired Suspense

Hiding in Plain Sight
Amish Holiday Vendetta
Deadly Amish Abduction

Justice Seekers

Soldier's Christmas Secrets
Guarded by the Soldier
Wyoming Mountain Escape
Hiding His Holiday Witness
Rocky Mountain Standoff
Fugitive Hunt

Rocky Mountain K-9 Unit

Hiding in Montana

Pacific Northwest K-9 Unit

Shielding the Baby

Visit the Author Profile page at LoveInspired.com for more titles.

Deadly Amish Abduction

Laura Scott

Love Inspired Suspense
Inspirational Romance

LOVE INSPIRED® SUSPENSE
INSPIRATIONAL ROMANCE

ISBN-13: 978-1-335-58775-6

Deadly Amish Abduction

Love Inspired
22 Adelaide St. West, 41st Floor
Toronto, Ontario M5H 4E3, Canada
www.LoveInspired.com

Printed in U.S.A.

He that dwelleth in the secret place of the most High shall abide under the shadow of the Almighty. I will say of the Lord, He is my refuge and my fortress: my God; in him will I trust. Surely he shall deliver thee from the snare of the fowler, and from the noisome pestilence.

—*Psalm* 91:1-3

This book is dedicated with love to my aunt Carolyn.
You are not only a great inspiration to me
but also one of the strongest women I know! I love you!

ONE

The stranger was standing outside her café again.

Rachel Miller, who owned and operated Rachel's Café in downtown Green Lake, Wisconsin, smiled and chatted as she served her customers, while surreptitiously watching the man loitering outside.

He was an *Englischer*, dressed in dark clothing and a baseball hat pulled low over his forehead. He was clean-shaven, but she knew that didn't mean much; it was only the Amish men who stopped shaving their beards once they were married. Her small dining room was full of customers, making it impossible for her to go outside to get a better look at him.

Yet his being there nagged at her. She was certain sure he'd been there for a while the day before, as well.

Was his presence outside her café a coincidence? It could be that the location was a designated meeting place. But there was something about the way he moved, and the way he kept his head down, that raised her suspicions.

She considered letting Liam Harland, the Green Lake

County sheriff, know about this man, but really, the stranger hadn't committed a crime. At least, not yet.

Mayhap he was thinking of trying to rob her. The thought made her angry, yet it was hard to imagine the small amount of cash she collected each day was worth his time and effort. The earnings were plentiful to her, as her needs were simple, but not to most in the *Englisch* world.

She hurried back to the kitchen to get soup and sandwiches for her newest customers. It wasn't easy doing both the cooking and the serving, but she preferred to handle everything herself. Besides, she only had room for six tables in her small café, so it wasn't as if she had enough business to support a full-time server. Often in the summer, which was the height of the tourist season, a few Amish teenage girls would come to help for a few hours.

When she returned with the two meals for her guests, the man was gone. Or at least, he wasn't standing in the same spot where she could see him through the window.

She sincerely doubted he was gone for good. The stranger was probably staying at one of the many rental vacation spots available in the Green Lake area. The May spring weather brought many tourists who enjoyed water sports on the lake and wandered around the quaint and picturesque town.

Rachel continued working, doing her best not to dwell on the stranger who'd lingered outside her café. She enjoyed mingling with her customers, hearing their plans as they spoke of the things they planned to do and to see. It was always amazing how many questions they had for her about being Amish.

Deep down, she was curious about them, too, largely because of her father. While she had no intention of leaving the community where she'd been born and raised, her father had gone back to the *Englisch* world, leaving her and her mother behind, when she was four years old. Rachel only had very vague memories about her father and since they didn't use electronics, she didn't have any photographs of him, either. When she was younger, she'd asked her mother about him and why he'd left, and her mother would only say he didn't want to be Amish anymore. She knew some chose to leave the community, but she sensed there was more to the story. She didn't ask anything more. Obviously, it was too painful for her mother to discuss the reasons her father had abandoned them.

Her mother, Arleta Miller, passed away last year after a long illness, leaving Rachel feeling at a crossroads. Bishop Bachman wanted her to find a suitor, reminding her of her duty to the Amish community, but Rachel wasn't in any hurry to marry and have children. Instead, she preferred pouring all her time and energy into her café.

Being a businesswoman provided her a sense of independence and accomplishment. She wasn't quite ready to give that up and feared any suitor would expect her to.

As the four-o'clock hour approached, her café customers dwindled away. She only served breakfast and the midday meal, which meant she was normally able to head home by five o'clock, after she'd cleaned the kitchen and dining area, and put everything away.

Most days, she lingered at the café, making something to eat for herself before leaving for the evening.

Certain sure she wasn't in a hurry to return to the empty house she'd shared with her *mammi*. Once again, she considered moving permanently to the small apartment above her café. The Amish elders wouldn't like it, fearing that her being so far away from their community would make her vulnerable to the *Englisch* ways.

Yet it would be nice not to have to walk back and forth from her house to the café each day. For now, she reserved her times for staying in the upstairs apartment for only those days that the weather was particularly bad.

The last pair of customers finally left at half past four. She quickly cleaned the main café area, then went back to the kitchen.

An hour later, she'd eaten her meal and had the kitchen spotless. The last thing she needed to do was haul the garbage out to the dumpster out back that she shared with the other shops located along Main Street.

The bag was heavy, but she managed to lift it with both hands. It took all her strength to fling the bag up and over the edge of the dumpster, where it landed softly on the other bags already in there.

A movement down the alley caught her eye, and she immediately tensed when she noticed a man standing near the side of the building. Dark clothes, dark baseball cap. The same stranger she'd seen outside her café earlier?

Raised voices reached her ears, and she frowned, realizing the man wasn't alone. She peeked around the edge of the dumpster to get a better view. There were two men standing roughly twenty feet away.

The man with the brown baseball cap and brown

jacket who'd been outside her café earlier, and another man. She turned away, then heard a grunt, then a soft thud as something fell.

She looked again and saw the man without a hat on holding a knife and standing over the other man, who was crumpled in a heap on the ground, groaning in pain. Even from this distance she could see blood pooling beneath him.

No! Rachel instinctively reared back in horror. Her elbow slammed into the side of the metal dumpster. The sound must have been loud enough to draw the knife man's attention because he turned to stare at her. She quickly ducked back inside the café, but then dashed through the building to head out the front door. She took a moment to lock it, then broke into a run.

Had the man with the knife gotten a good look at her face? The fact that she was dressed in Amish clothing would make it easy for him to find her. The café wasn't far from where the stabbing had happened. And it was the only Amish café in town.

What should she do? Notify the police? Seeking help from local law enforcement wasn't the Amish way, but this crime had occurred here in town, not within her community. A slight, but in this case notable, difference.

Her feet instinctively took her straight to the sheriff's department. At the very least, she could cut through the building, hopefully confusing the assailant should he try to find her.

The thought of walking all the way home alone was enough to make her shiver. The dark rain clouds swirling overhead made it seem later than it really was.

The people inside the sheriff's department all stared at her when she stepped inside. Amish didn't normally seek help from *Englisch* law enforcement. Ignoring the curious looks, she approached the deputy seated at the desk.

"May I please speak to Sheriff Liam?" She knew Liam Harland because he was her friend Elizabeth Walton's cousin, and because he often came to eat at her café. Liam's family had left the Amish when he was young, but he held them in high regard, and made a point of honoring their wishes.

Most of the time. He was still law enforcement, so he didn't appreciate not being informed of some of the crimes that took place within their Amish community.

"Sheriff Harland isn't here right now, but I can help you if you have a complaint?" The deputy eyed her curiously, no doubt wondering why an Amish woman would come to the police station at all.

"Ah, what about Chief Deputy Garrett Nichols? Is he here?"

"No, I'm afraid not." The guy frowned. "What do you need help with?"

She glanced over her shoulder, trying to decide what to do. Being inside the police station went against her beliefs. Yet she felt obligated to report the crime she'd witnessed. "I saw a man being stabbed," she finally admitted. "In the alley behind my café."

"Café? Oh, yes, you're Rachel Miller." The deputy frowned. "A man was stabbed? Are you sure?"

"I saw a man holding a knife, while the other man was lying on the ground, bleeding." She twisted her hands together nervously. “And I believe the assailant saw me, too.”

“Okay, take a seat. I’ll call Garrett and send a deputy over to investigate.” The deputy reached for the phone.

Stepping back, she bit her lip, trying to decide what to do. She’d done her duty by reporting the crime. Should she stay or go? The longer she waited, the darker it would become. She didn’t want to walk home in the rain.

If she left now, she could use the side door to leave the building, a tactic that may prevent the assailant from finding her.

Or mayhap not. What to do?

While the deputy was busy on the phone, she abruptly turned and hurried toward the side door. As she reached it, she heard the deputy calling to her, but she ignored him. Liam or Garrett would come find her tomorrow for more information, but for now, she couldn’t ignore the urge to get home.

As quickly as possible.

Rachel darted between cars in the parking lot located behind the sheriff’s department headquarters. She knew the general layout of the town and chose the shortest path to get her out to the main highway, which would take her to the Amish community.

A quick glance over her shoulder confirmed no one was behind her. At least not on foot. But there was traffic on the road, and she eyed every vehicle warily, fearing the assailant would be behind the wheel.

She alternated walking and running while searching for possible shortcuts. It was a bit too early in May for planting, so cutting through one of the farm fields was an option. Harder on her feet, but mayhap better in the long run.

Before she could make a move, she saw a horse-drawn buggy approaching. Someone from her community! Without hesitation, she lifted her arm and waved at the driver. "Help, please, help me!"

"Whoa, boy." The deep voice sounded familiar, and when the driver grew closer, she recognized Jacob Strauss. She saw him often enough at church services, but they hadn't spoken to each other since Elizabeth and David McKay's wedding two and a half months ago. He always came across as too somber and stuck in his ways. Likely due to the way he'd lost his wife and son two years ago.

"Rachel?" Jacob frowned. "Is something wrong?"

"*Ach*, Jacob, I need a ride home." She managed a strained smile. "Please?"

"Certain sure," he agreed. Even though he'd been headed in the opposite direction, he didn't seem to mind. He stood, offered his hand and helped her inside. "You appear upset. What is the problem?"

She dropped into the seat beside him, and let out a silent sigh of relief. Jacob didn't immediately turn around, as this stretch of road wasn't wide enough, but that was okay. This way she could see if anyone came to find her. She licked her lips and confessed, "I witnessed a man being stabbed not far from my café."

"An Amish man?" Jacob asked in shocked surprise.

She shook her head. "No, both men were *Englischers*. But I think the assailant saw me. As I'm obviously dressed as Amish, I've been worried that he may try to find me."

"Well, then you must stay away from the café." Jacob's authoritative tone irked her.

"No, Jacob, that's not possible. I have a business to run."

"And what if this assailant returns to find you in the morning? Then what?" he demanded.

Jacob's concern was not misplaced. He had a valid point. Yet she didn't have a good answer.

All she could do was bow her head, and pray for God to keep her safe.

Jacob glanced at Rachel, who appeared to be praying. He scowled, thinking of his deceased wife, Anna, and son, Isaac. God had not protected them, so why would He provide safety to Rachel?

He often wondered if Anna had intended to take Isaac, leaving him and the community. It's true she never expressed unhappiness during their marriage, but why else would they have been in their buggy so far outside the community? To an area where cars were not on the lookout for Amish buggies.

Shaking off the dour thoughts, he urged the horse into a trot, anxious to get Rachel home. First, though, he needed to reach the next intersection so they could turn around. They had experienced much rain recently, and more threatened from the overcast sky above. He didn't want to risk getting stuck in the mud along the sides of the road.

He didn't often go to the downtown area of Green Lake. Over the past few months, he'd come to understand that the Amish Shoppe—the large red barn that had been renovated to hold many smaller stores run by the Amish—and Rachel's Café provided well-needed funds to the community. Yet he didn't like the idea of their Amish women working among the *Englisch* outsiders. Anna had been content to stay home and to raise their son.

Yet after they'd died in the accident, he was forced to reconsider whether that was true. Was she leaving him personally? Or the Amish life in general? He did not know, but feared the former.

"I hope I'm not keeping you from something," Rachel said. "You must have been heading into town for a reason, *ja*?"

"Nothing pressing, certain sure." He didn't want to admit he'd taken the horse and buggy out because he needed to get away from the empty house for a while. As a farmer, he was normally busy, but it wasn't quite time to plant yet. Driving around without a destination wasn't the Amish way. They valued hard work and discipline, two things he normally excelled at.

However, his world had been shaken over the past few years. First when he'd lost his wife and son to a buggy accident, then again a few months ago when he'd learned the terrible truth about his best friend, Adam, who'd been dealing drugs to the *Englischers*.

The only good thing that had come out of that troubled time was that he'd helped save his neighbor Elizabeth from harm.

"How have you been?" Rachel's question had him glancing at her in surprise.

"Sehr gut," he answered automatically. Even though he was anything but good. He struggled to come up with safe topics of conversation, even though small talk

wasn't his strength. "I hear from Elizabeth and David that your café has been successful, *ain't so*?"

"Very much," she agreed with a smile. "I enjoy cooking and serving customers."

Joy brightened her face, and he secretly marveled at how pretty she was. Her dark hair was mostly hidden by her *kapp*, and her blue eyes were bright. She also had a small mole on the left side of her mouth. It was the first time he'd noticed a woman in the two years since Anna's passing, and wasn't sure why he was feeling this strange attraction now. It made him scowl. "I'm happy to hear that, but you must not return to the café tomorrow. I'm concerned about the danger."

Her expression turned serious. "*Ja*, me, too. But I have informed the sheriff's department. It's their job to enforce the *Englisch* laws, *ain't so*? Certain sure they'll find the assailant soon enough."

By tomorrow? Somehow he didn't think so, although there was no denying the local authorities were good at their jobs. He wouldn't normally interact with them, but just before Christmas Liam Harland had arrested Adam's cousin for attempted murder of David, a former *Englischer* who was now baptized Amish. David and Elizabeth were now happily married and active members of their Amish community.

"We'll turn around up ahead, *ja*?" He gestured to the intersection in the road.

"Sehr gut."

A dark blue truck came toward them. He slowed the horse, pulling over to the side of the road to give the driver more room, but to his surprise, the vehicle slowed, too, as it approached.

Rachel grabbed his arm. "Jacob, that may be the man with the knife," she whispered.

"I know." He didn't increase his pace, pretending they were an Amish couple with nothing to hide, heading into town. He was glad he hadn't found a place to turn around earlier; hopefully the fact that they were headed toward town, rather than away, would help fool the driver. He knew many of the *Englisch* thought all Amish looked the same.

Rachel buried her face against his shoulder. He pasted a nonchalant expression on his face as he patted her arm reassuringly. The driver of the truck seemed to look directly at him, then eventually passed by without incident.

He waited another few minutes to make sure the driver was truly gone. "I think you're okay now, Rachel."

She lifted her head and gazed up at him for a moment. "*Denke*, Jacob."

"Wilkom." He didn't appreciate how much he'd enjoyed her leaning on him. Scowling again, he pulled back on the reins, and turned the buggy around at the intersection. Soon they were heading back toward the Amish community.

"I may have overreacted," Rachel said after a long moment. "Mayhap that was not the man I saw in the alley."

"And mayhap it was." He winced at his blunt tone. "Rachel, but you must stay home for a few days. Certain sure Liam will let you know when they have the assailant behind bars."

She didn't answer, and he decided not to push it. He'd

said his piece; it was up to Rachel to use her common sense and listen to reason.

They rode in silence for several long moments. Up ahead, he noticed another vehicle coming down the highway toward them. His gaze narrowed as it drew closer.

It was a blue truck. The same one from before.

"Jacob, he's back!" Rachel cried.

He tugged on the reins, taking the buggy as far over to the side of the road as possible. As before, the truck slowed down. Only this time, the driver's side window slowly opened.

A gun!

TWO

Rachel gripped Jacob's arm tightly, praying for God to find a way for them to get away. A horse and buggy couldn't outrun a car.

Or avoid a gun.

"Hiya!" Jacob slapped the reins, urging the horse to go faster. "Go!"

"Pull over!" the man behind the wheel shouted. "Or I'll shoot!"

"Please, Lord, save us!" The words burst from her throat even as Jacob ignored the command to pull over. "Hurry," she urged as they passed the car.

She'd braced for gunfire, but didn't hear it. Seconds later, tires squealed as the driver of the truck abruptly hit the brakes. She couldn't see what was going on behind them, but felt certain the truck would turn around, coming up behind them. Chasing them.

Or maybe the driver would simply start shooting.

"I'm sorry, Jacob," she whispered. "So sorry."

"We're not dead yet. Hiya! Giddyap!"

As if sensing the danger, the horse went faster, moving from a trot to a gallop. The increased speed sent the buggy rocking back and forth—it wasn't designed to be used in a race. She clung to Jacob's arm with one hand, the other gripping the seat.

The rumble of an engine grew louder. The truck wasn't that far behind them now, and she felt certain bullets would fly any second.

When they reached the next intersection, though, the truck abruptly backed off. It took her a moment to understand that a tan-colored sheriff's deputy vehicle was coming toward them from the right.

She instinctively raised her arm to get the attention of the deputy. The squad car slowed, and as they flew past, she caught a glimpse of a familiar face behind the wheel. Not Liam, but Garrett.

The truck backed off, tires squealing as it made yet another U-turn. The buggy rocked so erratically, she feared it would flip over.

"Whoa," Jacob said, lightly pulling back on the reins to bring the buggy to normal speeds. She could feel the tense muscles in his arms as he fought to control the horse.

"Is the truck gone?" she asked.

"*Ja*. But the deputy is coming up behind us." Jacob glanced at her. "Certain sure you want to talk to him?"

"I do. The man with a gun needs to be caught, *ain't so*?"

Jacob's scowl deepened, but he didn't argue. Mayhap the close call had shaken him as much as it had her.

The horse slowly returned to a walk, then stopped, his sides still heaving with exertion. She forced herself to release her deathlike grip on Jacob's arm so that he could hop down to tend to the animal.

Jacob held out his hand to help her down, too. She accepted his support, her knees still wobbly from the terrifying event.

"Rachel, what's going on?" Garrett asked. He'd parked his squad car and hurried over. "Why were you going so fast?"

"*Ach*, did you see the dark blue truck behind us?" she asked. "The driver had a gun, and demanded we pull over."

"A gun?" Garrett whipped around to stare at the stretch of highway behind them. His expression was grim as he turned back to face her. "I saw the truck turn around, but I didn't realize you were trying to escape from it. I thought maybe something spooked your horse."

She shook her head. Jacob remained with the horse, soothing the animal after their wild ride. "It was the same man who stabbed the stranger in the alley behind the café."

"Stabbed a stranger?" Garrett narrowed his gaze. "Maybe you should start at the beginning."

"We need to get home." Jacob spoke up for the first time. "Before the truck returns."

Garrett sighed, then nodded. "Okay, but I'm going to escort you back to the Amish community. When you're safe there, I'd like to hear exactly what happened."

She was glad Jacob nodded in agreement, a big step for the man so set in his ways. She smiled gratefully. "*Denke*, Jacob. I appreciate your willingness to assist."

"I want you to be safe, Rachel." He moved back to the buggy and quickly jumped in. Then he held out his hand for her. "*Komm.* The sooner we get to my farm, the better."

After he helped her up, they took their seats. There was no reason now to hold on to his arm, but she was surprised by the urge to do so. She slipped her hand over his forearm, needing this brief connection while half expecting him to shake it off. Yet he didn't seem to notice.

Her house wasn't that far from Jacob's farm. She was not surprised, though, when Jacob pulled into his driveway before going on to her home. Certain sure he'd want to take care of his horse after pushing the animal so hard.

To protect her. She was humbled by Jacob's determination to shield her from harm. Mayhap he was only protecting himself, too, but she didn't think so.

"Go inside the house," Jacob said, after helping her down from the buggy. "I'll take care of the horse while you talk to the deputy."

"Do you need help?" She didn't have much experience in caring for horses but felt the need to offer anyway.

"No, just go inside." He was back to being his usual curt self. No doubt he didn't want much to do with *Englisch* law enforcement.

She left him at the barn, hurrying over to meet with Garrett, who was standing beside his squad car. "*Komm*, we'll go inside to talk, *ja*?"

This wasn't the first time she'd been inside Jacob's home. He'd hosted church services about ten weeks ago, but it still felt strange to be there alone, well, except for Garrett. She removed her cloak and took a moment to add wood to the stove before taking a seat on the sofa next to Garrett.

"I saw a stranger loitering outside my café, yesterday and today," she said slowly. "He wore a brown shirt, and a brown baseball hat pulled low, so I didn't get a very clear look at his face. I was busy with customers when I noticed him today, and the next time I glanced over, he was gone."

"Go on," Garrett encouraged.

"After I closed for the evening, I took the garbage out back and heard raised voices followed by a thud. Peering around the edge of the dumpster, I saw a man holding a knife, while the man in the ball cap was lying on the ground groaning in pain."

"He stabbed him?" Garrett asked.

"Ja." She took a moment to gather herself. "When I hit my elbow against the edge of the dumpster, the assailant looked over and saw me."

"Can you describe him?"

She thought back for a moment. "Brown hair streaked with gray, and a clean-shaven face. *Ach*, I'm sorry I can't be more precise. It all happened so fast, and both times, outside the café and again as he drove the truck, I only caught a passing glance."

Jacob came inside through the back door. He walked through the kitchen and joined them in the living room.

Garrett turned toward him. "Jacob, did you get a good look at the gunman?"

Jacob hesitated, as if debating whether to cooperate with the police investigation. Then he glanced at her. "Brown hair with gray at the temples, and clean-shaven, as Rachel said. He was wearing a black shirt, but otherwise, I was focused on the gun in his hand."

"What type of gun?" Garrett wanted to know.

Jacob shook his head. "I'm not familiar with handguns."

"I'm not, either," she added. "But he didn't shoot when he had the chance. He demanded we pull over."

Garrett's eyebrows hiked up at that bit of news. "Any idea why he would do that?"

"Mayhap because he wanted me to go with him?" The interaction had bothered her, as it didn't make any sense. "The only thing I can come up with is that he wasn't completely sure I was the woman who witnessed what happened in the alley."

"Why didn't you call 911 after the stabbing?" Garrett asked, looking frustrated.

"I ran to the sheriff's department to report the event," she informed him. "I asked for Liam and for you, but you weren't there. The deputy at the desk made some calls, and I decided to leave before it got too dark outside. I didn't want to be caught in the storm."

"If I hadn't been out in the buggy, the gunman would have her by now." Jacob frowned. "*Ach*, it's important for you to find that dark blue truck."

"I'm on it," Garrett assured him. "You didn't by chance get a license plate number?"

"No, I didn't." She looked at Jacob, who also shook his head. "Again, it all happened very fast."

"I understand." Garrett stood. "I need to discuss this with Liam. I take it you're not going to open the café tomorrow."

"I must open the café," she protested. "How will I support myself if I don't?"

Jacob's scowl deepened, and Garrett looked just as frustrated. She hated disappointing them both, but what choice did she have.

"You need to stay hidden for a few days, while Liam and I figure out who this guy is," Garrett said firmly. "You know he'll find you at the café, Rachel."

"What am I supposed to do? Sit home alone all day?" She couldn't imagine doing nothing.

"You will stay here." Jacob's authoritative tone grated on her nerves. "I will keep you safe."

"That would be improper." She looked back at Garrett. "I will consider staying home for a few days, but no longer. You must find this man, quickly."

"That's the goal." Garrett moved toward the door. "Oh, and, Rachel? I understand you being here with Jacob goes against the Amish rules, but you really shouldn't be alone until we get this guy behind bars."

She sighed and rubbed her temple as Garrett left. Deep down, she didn't want to stay alone.

But staying with Jacob would be akin to claiming him as her suitor. She would not ruin his good name, or hers. She stood and headed toward the door. "I must head home, but please know I appreciate everything you've done for me, Jacob. It's only because of your strength and determination, and God's protection, that we were able to escape."

Jacob lifted his hat and threaded his fingers through his thick, wavy dark brown hair. "I'll escort you home."

"Denke." She hesitated, glancing at his kitchen. She didn't see anything resembling the evening meal. "Have

you eaten? Certain sure I can make something before I go."

"No, I haven't eaten." His expression was guarded, but he must have been hungry, because he gestured toward the kitchen. "I would very much enjoy a meal, if you can find something to make."

"*Ach*, is that a challenge I hear?" She grinned and nodded. "*Sehr gut.* I'm sure I'll find something to make for dinner."

Cooking for Jacob was the least she could do to repay him for saving her life.

And she was secretly glad to be with him, even if only for a short while longer.

Jacob watched Rachel bustle around in his kitchen with mixed emotions. It had been a long time since a woman had cooked for him. He'd come to prefer his solitary existence, avoiding memories of Anna and Isaac, yet this evening, he didn't mind spending more time with Rachel.

She hummed one of the popular church hymns as she worked. He wondered if she was always this cheerful, and if so, why? Rachel lived alone, as he did.

Certain sure he'd never in his life hummed while he worked. Not even when Anna and Isaac were still alive.

Normally thinking about his wife and son made his chest hurt, but today he was distracted by the dark-haired independent Amish woman who had witnessed a crime and invited the *Englischer* deputy into his home.

Not to mention, the scent of her cooking.

By the time she was finished, he could barely contain his hunger. "*Komm*, Jacob. We'll say grace, *ja*?"

He bowed his head, and tried not to react when she took his hand. For a moment his mind went blank, but then he managed to regain his senses. "Lord, we ask You to bless this food and to keep Rachel safe in Your care. Amen."

"Amen," Rachel echoed. She squeezed his hand, then released it. He was shocked at how his fingers tingled from her touch. "I feel I should apologize for placing you in danger, too."

"No need, I was happy to have been there for you." He tried to smile. "I'm glad you're safe."

"Me, too." She beamed at him, and he found himself flustered by her expression. Why was she so happy? Shouldn't she be upset about being followed by a gunman? "*Ach*, you're not eating."

He quickly took a bite. "*Denke*, Rachel, you're a very good cook."

"My customers seem to think so," she responded modestly. Pride wasn't favored by the Amish, and she quickly changed the subject. "I know you will be upset with me, but I'd really like to open the café tomorrow."

And just like that, his mood turned sour. "Why? To invite trouble?"

"I knew you'd say that." She sighed. "What would you do, if the situation was reversed? Would you hide out here on the farm?"

"I would not run a café in town," he shot back. "It's too far away and invites danger from outsiders."

"*Ach*, don't be so grumpy." She sounded exasperated with him. "God has blessed me with the ability to cook—certain sure He would not want me to waste it.

And others work at the Amish Shoppe, which isn't that much different, *ain't so*?"

He had no idea how to respond to that, so he focused on eating. The woman was maddening, and clearly didn't care what he thought.

He wasn't her suitor, so she really wasn't his problem to deal with. Yet he couldn't deny the need to keep her safe from harm. When the gunman had opened his truck window, Jacob had done his best to shield her with his body, expecting to feel the painful impact of a bullet ripping into him.

He still wasn't sure how they'd managed to escape being killed. The man could have shot him, or the horse, and taken Rachel with him, if that was his intent.

The thought sent an icy finger of fear down his spine.

"If you insist on going to the café tomorrow, then I'm going with you."

She lifted a brow. "*Ach*, a ride would be nice, but there's no need for you to stay, Jacob."

"There's every need." The words came out harsher than he intended. Elizabeth had warned him about being so blunt, so he did his best to backtrack. "You must realize the gunman is likely to come to the café."

Rachel frowned, dropping her gaze from his. "I believe Garrett and Liam will be watching for that possibility."

Leaving her safety in the hands of outsiders was not an option. "Mayhap you are right, but that's even more reason for me to be there, too."

She nodded, but didn't say anything for a long moment. "If I don't go to the café, then I fear the gunman will come here to our community." She finally lifted her gaze to meet his. "Don't you see, Jacob? I don't want to be responsible for placing others in harm's way."

"The blame is not yours, Rachel." He sighed and added, "And if you won't stay here with me, will you consider going to Elizabeth's? I'm sure she and David would allow you to stay."

"I don't want them to be in danger, either." A small smile played along her mouth. "I recently learned Elizabeth may be expecting, so staying with her and David and *Mammi* Ruth is not an option."

He hadn't known the couple was expecting, but he was truly happy for them. David and Elizabeth deserved to be blessed in such a way.

Yet that still left him with no option other than to escort Rachel home.

He quickly finished his meal. Rachel jumped up from her seat. "I'll wash the dishes first, then head home, *ja*?"

Humbled by her offer, he managed a nod, then headed out to bring in more firewood. More for something to do than out of need. It occurred to him that she might need help with getting wood for her stove, and silently promised to take on that chore for her.

When she was finished, he reached for his coat, then held her cloak for her.

"Denke." She sounded breathless as he draped the cape around her slim shoulders.

They stepped outside. The temperature remained in the midsixties, and he was relieved to note the rain hadn't started yet. It would soon, though; the air was heavy with moisture.

Neither of them spoke as they walked the distance

between his farm and her small house. He tried to think of something to say, but he was out of practice.

Once he'd courted Anna, convincing her to marry him. He glanced at Rachel, wondering why she didn't have suitors lined up. Likely because she seemed intent on running her café, more so than settling down.

"*Ach*, here we are." She gestured toward the house. "I appreciate you walking me home."

"I'll chop more wood for your stove." He'd noticed her woodpile was getting low. "Go inside. I'll be in shortly."

"There's no need," she protested.

"You cooked for me," he interjected. "This is my way of returning the favor." He swiftly walked to the woodpile, picked up the axe and went to work.

The physical labor felt good. Strange, because it was just another chore when he did it for himself. Yet he had a newfound energy this evening, knowing he was helping Rachel.

When he'd finished the two logs that were lying there, he made a mental note to bring more wood over later. He gathered a large pile of split logs in his arms, and walked up to the house. He rapped on the door with his elbow, and she quickly opened the door for him.

"*Denke*, Jacob." Rachel smiled and gestured toward the wood-burning stove in the corner of the room.

He took a moment to stack the wood, then feed the stove. When he'd dawdled as long as he could, he rose and turned to face her.

"Are you sure about staying here alone?" He felt obligated to try one last time. "No one needs to know I slept on your sofa. We know there's nothing improper and isn't anyone else's business, *ain't so*?"

"You know how information tends to get out. Some people love nothing more than to discuss others, *ja*? Truly, I'll be fine, Jacob." She looked at him for a long moment, as if there was more she wanted to say, but then she crossed to the door. "I'll see you in the morning."

He was shocked at how badly he wanted to stay. So much so, that he had to force himself to leave. Finally, he opened the front door, glancing at her over his shoulder. "Good night, Rachel."

"Good night, Jacob."

He stepped outside. She closed the door, but he didn't immediately walk away. He stood there, trying to come up with a way to convince Rachel to let him stay.

The clouds above opened and rain fell in sheets upon his head. He wore his hat, but even so, the water seeped down the back of his neck.

By the time he made it back to his house, he was soaked through to the skin. Something that would normally annoy him, but not tonight.

For the first time in the past two years, he looked forward to what tomorrow might bring.

Because he planned to stick to Rachel like glue, until the gunman was arrested and tossed in jail.

THREE

As the rain pounded against the roof, Rachel tried to sleep. But the late-afternoon events swirled in her mind. A man had been stabbed right in front of her eyes. It was difficult to erase the memory.

The slightest sounds jerked her awake, her heart pounding in fear that the gunman may have found her.

By morning, her nerves were frayed. Should she go to the café, or stay home? Staying home might be safer, but for how long? Keeping her café closed indefinitely would likely cause her to lose much of her business. It wouldn't take long for customers to go elsewhere for a meal.

She bowed her head and prayed for guidance. Much of the tension melted away, and Rachel knew she'd go to the café. The gunman wasn't likely to walk into the crowded café to do her harm.

No, the most dangerous part of her day would be going to and from the café.

After washing up and donning a fresh dress and apron, she pulled on her *kapp* and walked to the door.

She normally didn't break her fast at home, preferring to eat at the café before she opened for business.

The rain from the night before had ended, but the ground was still damp and muddy. Lifting her skirt, she stepped outside.

The snorting sound of a horse had her turning toward the road. Jacob was coming toward her in his buggy, his expression grim. He would be a handsome man if he would smile more, although she understood he was still mourning the loss of his family.

"Good morning, Rachel." He greeted her cordially enough, although she fully expected a lecture. "I hope you slept well."

"Ja, sehr gut." It wasn't true, but she didn't want to admit how scared she'd been.

Jacob stood and offered his hand. She accepted his help getting into the buggy, praying they didn't run into the blue truck again.

"I will take a different route to town," Jacob said as he steered the horse onto the side of the road. "It will take longer, but mayhap be safer, *ja*?"

"Sehr gut." She couldn't argue with his plan, although it would be nice if he asked for her input rather than flat out telling her. "I must be there by six o'clock to have time to prepare."

"Hiya!" Jacob urged the horse into a trot, then glanced at her. "I will make sure we get there in time."

"Denke." She smiled. "And if you haven't had time to break your fast, I shall make breakfast for you when we get there."

His stern expression brightened and he nodded. "I would appreciate a meal."

"I'm sure you must get back to the farm, afterward." She had never lived on a farm, but had a vague memory of neighbors who'd worked hard with the animals.

"I've taken care of the morning chores already," Jacob said. "There is no rush for me to get back."

She felt guilty knowing he must have been up well before dawn to have accomplished that work. "You don't have to drive me each day—certain sure I can walk."

"No walking alone until this man is caught."

She bristled at his terse tone. "Are you asking me or telling me?" She turned in her seat. "I don't appreciate you barking orders."

He clenched his jaw for a moment, then said, "Rachel, will you please allow me to drive you each day until the gunman is caught?"

"*Ja*, I would very much appreciate a ride, *denke*." She patted his arm. "There, now, was that so difficult?"

His eyebrows shot up at her comment, but then the corner of his mouth quirked in a rare smile. "I will try to remember not to bark orders."

"Sehr gut." She kept a keen eye on the road, watching for the blue truck. Mayhap Garrett and Liam had already found the driver, and the danger was already over. She hoped one of them would come to the café to provide an update, although she could also stop over to talk to them in person after she closed for the day.

When they arrived at the café without running across the gunman, she felt certain sure he was already in police custody. Jacob pulled up near the front of her café, then helped her down.

"Please, come inside, *ja*? The horse will be okay for a short while."

"I'll find a place to secure him." Jacob waited for her to unlock the front door of the café before leading the horse down Main Street.

She headed into the kitchen to begin their meals. She heard the door chime. Poking her head out through the opening between the kitchen and the dining room, she saw Jacob standing there. He seemed curious about her café, as he'd never been there before. "Have a seat. I'll be finished shortly."

He nodded and pulled out a chair at one of the tables that had a direct line of sight to the front door.

Today she was making French toast with thick cuts of sourdough bread. She added some bacon to the fry pan, then carried a pot of coffee out to the dining room.

"Would you like some?" she asked.

He nodded. "This is very nice."

She could feel her cheeks grow pink and tried to remember that pride and boasting was a sin. "*Denke*, Jacob." She finished pouring his coffee, then returned to the kitchen.

A few minutes later, she brought out two plates of food. After setting one down in front of Jacob, she took the seat across from him. "Would you like to say grace?"

He hesitated, then bowed his head. "Lord, we thank You for this food we are about to eat. And we ask that You keep Rachel safe in Your care, amen."

"Amen." She frowned. "*Ach*, you should have included your safety, too, Jacob. I would not want you to be harmed because of me."

"Because of the gunman," he corrected. "An *Englischer* with evil in his heart."

"Certain sure Garrett and Liam have arrested him by now." She downplayed the danger, as there was nothing she could do to change the situation. "I hope the meal is to your liking."

He took a moment to eat, then nodded. "*Sehr gut.* I can see why your business is so successful."

It was the nicest thing he'd ever said to her, and she wanted to hug him for the kind words. But of course, she didn't. Jacob might be providing her rides to and from the café, but she knew he was still very set in his ways. Mayhap if things were different…

No, what was she thinking? She wasn't interested in Jacob, or in courting in general. Jacob was too grouchy and too fond of issuing orders. Besides, the moment they knew the gunman had been captured, things between them would return to normal.

They didn't talk much as they ate. She kept an eye on the time, knowing she needed to have things ready to go once she opened for business.

When they were finished, she took the dishes back to the kitchen. She expected Jacob would head home, so she didn't bother to return with more coffee. When she had the dishes washed, and the breakfast food prepped and ready to go, she went back to the dining room, stopping abruptly when she saw Jacob still sitting there.

"*Ach*, I thought you left," she said in surprise. "The horse needs tending, *ain't so*?"

He inclined his head. "*Ja*, but I don't want to leave you alone." He gestured to his empty coffee cup. "*Mayhap* I could have more?"

"Of course." Flustered, she quickly refilled his cup. "But, Jacob, you can't stay here all day." She didn't want to sound ungrateful, but she'd need the table to fill with those who would buy a meal.

"Just until customers arrive, *ja*?" He sipped his coffee.

She frowned, then walked over to the door. She turned the Closed sign to Open, and then began to set the tables, using quilted place mats made by Elizabeth McKay. As she worked, she was keenly aware of Jacob's intense gaze, watching her.

The man was an enigma, certain sure. When the door chimed, she glanced over. Liam Harland was dressed in full uniform, and he nodded at Jacob then turned to her. "Rachel, I would love breakfast."

She had to smile, as Liam was a frequent visitor to her café. "Of course, please take a seat. I'll bring you coffee, *ja*?"

Liam went over to sit with Jacob, his gaze following her. "I understand you witnessed a stabbing yesterday."

She nodded. "And the man who committed the crime drives a dark blue truck. He tried to pull Jacob over at gunpoint on the way home."

"Garrett told me." Liam frowned. "We haven't found the man who was stabbed."

She blinked. "You haven't?"

"No. There's blood in the alley, so I believe your story about what took place, but we don't know where the victim is. He could still be alive, or he could be dead."

Her knees threatened to buckle, so she dropped into the chair nearest Jacob. To her surprise he reached out to take her hand. "I assume you've checked the local hospitals?"

"Yes, but so far we don't have anything. A knife wound is a mandatory report to the police, so if he does seek medical help we'll know. In the meantime we're still searching for the dark blue truck. Unfortunately, we haven't found anything on that yet."

No victim, no blue truck. The news was staggering.

"What does this mean, Liam?" Jacob asked.

Liam sighed and rubbed the back of his neck. "It means Rachel is still in danger. But don't worry, we're going to have a deputy keeping an eye on this place until we know more."

Rachel exchanged concerned looks with Jacob. This was not the news she wanted to hear. Yet she couldn't help but wonder if the lack of a victim might work in her favor.

Liam's deputies hadn't found the blue truck, and while there were some tourists around town, it wasn't the height of the season, so finding the truck shouldn't be difficult.

It made her believe the gunman had decided to leave town. The man who'd been stabbed could be in the back of the truck, or dumped in the lake. Either way, she couldn't be a witness to a crime that didn't have a victim.

Could she?

Jacob didn't like what he was hearing from Liam, and knew Rachel felt the same. Her hand in his radiated warmth, and he was reluctant to let her go.

"You mentioned keeping an eye on Rachel's Café, but what does that mean? Having someone sitting inside all day?" he asked.

"Probably not all day, but I'm here for breakfast and Garrett plans to stop in for lunch." Liam glanced at Rachel. "When you're finished here at the end of the day, we'd like you to work with a sketch artist to give us an idea of what this guy looks like."

Her hand tightened in his. "I can try, but it happened very fast."

"I can do that," Jacob said. "I saw his face, too, *ja*?"

"That would be great." Liam offered a wry smile. "That should help us find this guy."

"If he's here to find," Rachel said.

Liam nodded. "It's possible he took off, but somehow I don't think so. I find it hard to believe he showed up here, stabbed a man, then left town. Why did he come in the first place?"

The tiny bell over Rachel's door chimed. She pulled her hand from his and stood. "Excuse me, I must get breakfast started."

Jacob watched her greet the new customers with a smile. Her positive attitude was amazing considering the depressing news Liam had shared.

The way Rachel put her troubles aside was humbling. He realized he'd let losing Anna and Isaac define him in a less than positive way.

"Jacob, I need a favor," Liam said, breaking into his troubled thoughts.

He was instantly wary, especially as he didn't normally interact with *Englisch* law enforcement. Well, back at Christmas he had, but that situation was different. "What sort of favor?"

"I saw your horse and buggy outside, I'd like one of

my deputies to escort you home, then give you a ride back."

"Why?" Jacob didn't understand the point.

"I'd like you and Rachel to work with the sketch artist at the end of the day, and then I'll drive you both home afterward. It will be safer than you taking the buggy back and forth."

He mulled over Liam's offer. He hadn't ridden in a car since he was sixteen, enjoying his *rumspringa*, but that wasn't what held him back. He shared Liam's goal in keeping Rachel safe. And had planned to stay close.

But he also had farm animals to care for, and equipment to repair. The planting season would start in another week and he needed to be ready. There was also the sense he'd gotten from Rachel that she didn't want him sitting in the café, taking up one of her tables all day, either.

"I have a favor in return." Jacob finished his coffee, setting the cup aside. "I will accept the escort home, *denke*, but need some time to work with the livestock before returning. It would work better for you or another member from your law enforcement team to return in the midafternoon to pick me up."

"That sounds reasonable." Liam smiled wryly. "I will do my best to keep Rachel safe while she's working, but I sense that she will be fine with a café full of customers."

Jacob nodded, hoping Liam was correct.

Rachel brought Liam's breakfast, and he watched as the sheriff bowed his head to pray before eating. He dropped his gaze, thinking the *Englischer* was a good man, despite not being Amish. Painful to admit he wouldn't have prayed without Rachel's insistence.

More customers came in, and Rachel hurried over to greet them. He was impressed at how she seemed to thrive here, and at the kind way she smiled and chatted while serving her patrons. After tasting her cooking, certain sure he understood why the café was so popular.

Yet he still felt as if a woman's place was tending to the home. Not running a business, especially so far away from their community. He wanted to tell her that the location of her café likely brought criminals to her establishment, but knew all too well that criminal minds were everywhere.

Even among the Amish.

After Liam finished eating, he paid Rachel and led the way outside. Jacob released his horse, and jumped back up into the buggy.

Having Liam's squad car keeping a slow pace behind him the entire way home was very unusual. But once he was back at the farm, he quickly went to work.

The horses and cattle were his top priority. It occurred to him that Ezekiel Moore and others would pitch in to help if he should ask.

Something he'd never done, not even after losing Anna and Isaac. Certain sure the women had rallied to provide him meals, but he had welcomed the hard work of running his farm and hadn't taken anyone up on offers to help.

He told himself that Liam and Garrett would find the dark blue truck very soon, so there would be no need to ask for help.

The hours passed quickly. When he was finished

for the day, he washed up and headed back outside to wait for Liam.

A large vehicle approached, causing him to tense. Had the gunman gotten a different car to use? But then he recognized Liam's face behind the wheel and realized he'd come in his private car, rather than one of the squad cars from the sheriff's department.

It was a kind gesture, as the Amish didn't like dealing with the police, preferring to handle any criminal behavior on their own. Yet over the past few months, there had been more vehicles than normal coming through their community, thanks to several dangerous incidents that had transpired over the past nine months.

And now Rachel had gotten herself involved in yet another *Englisch* criminal investigation. So much danger had come to their otherwise quiet and serene community.

"Rachel is fine," Liam said as he slid into the passenger seat. "I checked on her before coming out. Sounds like she had a steady stream of business today."

"*Denke*, that is good to hear." He glanced around the interior of the car, taking note of the technology that lit up the dashboard.

"Jacy Urban is our sketch artist. We share her services with the police department in Oshkosh. I'm going to take you straight to the station to work with her."

"Sehr gut," he agreed.

The ride didn't take long via car, and Jacob hated to admit it was nice to get back and forth so quickly. Not that he planned to change his ways. He followed Liam inside the sheriff's department headquarters and was introduced to a woman roughly his age of twenty-five with short blond hair.

"Okay, Jacob, let's get started." Jacy smiled and picked up her sketch pad.

He gave her credit for not gawking at him, the way many *Englischers* did. And there was no denying she was a skilled artist. After answering her numerous questions and making several tweaks to the drawing, she finally gestured to the sketch they'd completed.

The result was eerily accurate. "That's him." There was no doubt in his mind.

"Great." Jacy tore the sketch off and rose. "I'll get this to Liam, and he'll get this scanned into the computer and sent to all the deputies."

He didn't know anything about computers, but nodded in agreement. "Does this mean you don't need Rachel's help?"

Liam came over to join them. "I'd like Rachel to come in. She may remember a detail or two that you missed."

"Okay, I'll escort her here when she's finished." Jacob turned to leave.

The moment he stepped outside, he noticed the wind had picked up. The temperature had dropped a bit, too. There weren't as many people walking around now as there had been in the morning. Mayhap due to the change in weather. Wisconsin weather could be fickle, he knew. Which is why he generally waited until late May to do his planting.

He walked quickly down to the café, noting the Closed sign had been put on the front door. He checked the door handle, a bit surprised to find it unlocked.

Locking doors wasn't usual within their community,

but here he'd expected her to keep it locked. Especially after the incident with the gunman.

He stepped inside, the tinkle of the bell announcing his presence.

"Jacob? Is that you?"

"Ja." He almost chastised her for keeping the door unlocked, but managed to hold back. Certain sure she would not appreciate a scolding.

"I'm almost ready," she called back. "I just need to take the garbage out."

In the same alley where she'd witnessed the stabbing? "No!" His voice was sharp. "You will not take the garbage out."

Rachel poked her head through the doorway, a scowl etched on her face. "*Certain sure* I told you I don't appreciate you barking orders."

She disappeared before he could say anything more. Muttering under his breath about the stubbornness of business owners, he strode through the café and entered the kitchen.

The back door was open and there was no sign of Rachel. He hurried over to see her tossing a bag of garbage up and into the dumpster.

Out of nowhere, a white vehicle pulled up and a man jumped out from the back seat. He threw a hood over Rachel's head and jerked her toward the car.

"No! Stop!" Jacob lunged forward, grabbing the edge of the door before the guy could close it. Then he grabbed on to Rachel's arm. "Let her go!"

The man inside abruptly shoved Rachel toward him as the driver hit the gas. Jacob managed to pull Rachel out of harm's way seconds before the vehicle peeled away through the alley.

He clutched her against him, his heart thudding painfully against his ribs as he realized how close Rachel had come to being kidnapped.

FOUR

Without Jacob's strong arms holding Rachel upright, she'd have collapsed on the ground. She pushed the hood off her head with shaky fingers.

The gunman had tried to kidnap her!

"Let's get you inside." Jacob urged her toward the door leading into the back of her kitchen. Once there, he turned and locked the door. He held her shoulders and looked down at her. "Are you hurt?"

"I— No." The gunman had hit her head against the edge of the car, but she didn't mention it. "Thank you, Jacob."

His jaw tightened with anger, and she knew what he would say before the words left his lips. "I told you it was not safe for you to be here. If you had closed the café and stayed home this wouldn't have happened."

"You are right." She was too shaken to argue. "Although in truth, I was fine until I took out the garbage."

"He almost kidnapped you!"

"I know. I'm sorry." Tears pricked her eyes. Never would she have imagined the gunman would come around back, attempting to force her into his vehicle.

"*Ach*, Rachel." Jacob's anger faded as he pulled her close. "I'm glad you're not hurt."

She leaned against him for a moment, still trying to come to grips with what had happened.

"Stay here, I will fetch your *kapp*." Jacob loosened his grip and stepped back. She lifted a hand to her hair, realizing she must have dislodged her head covering when she'd taken the hood off.

Jacob unlocked the door, peered into the alley, then ran out to grab the item. He brought her missing *kapp* inside, then relocked the door.

"We will give this to Liam, *ja*?" Jacob handed her the *kapp*, then took the hood from her fingers. Just seeing it made her shiver.

"Sehr gut," she whispered. Turning away, she pulled her *kapp* over her hair, tucking in the loose strands that had become dislodged. Her fingers trembled, making it difficult to complete the task.

Jacob drew her toward the front door. He hesitated, then turned to look down at her. "The sheriff's department isn't far—are you ready to head over there?"

As ready as she'd ever be, she thought, but gave a nod. "Of course. Liam will want to know about this incident, *ain't so*?"

Jacob's brow furrowed. "You agreed to work with the sketch artist, too, remember?"

"*Ach*, yes. I remember." She drew in a deep breath to settle her nerves. "That should be fine."

Yet deep down, her stomach remained tied in knots. What if Jacob hadn't been there? She'd have been taken away in the gunman's car and likely killed.

All because she'd witnessed a crime.

"Stay beside me." Jacob's deep voice interrupted her thoughts. He opened the front door and took a step outside. After glancing around, he drew her out, too.

She quickly locked the door behind her, then followed him as Jacob made his way down and across the street to the sheriff's department headquarters.

Twice in twenty-four hours, she thought as they entered the building. The entire scenario was difficult to comprehend. How had this happened? How had her normal, routine life taken such a drastic turn?

Why, Lord, why?

"We are here to see Jacy Urban," Jacob announced. "And we need to speak with Sheriff Harland, as well."

"This way," the deputy said, opening a door that led to the office area.

Jacob kept her hand in his as they followed the deputy. They were escorted to a work space where a pretty blonde *Englisch* woman sat holding a sketch pad.

"Are you Rachel Miller? I'm Jacy, nice to meet you." Jacy stood, then gestured to the chair across from her. "Please have a seat."

Rachel reluctantly released Jacob's hand. She hadn't realized how much she'd depended on his strength and support. *"Denke,"* she whispered, taking the seat across from Jacy. "It's nice to meet you, too."

"I will find Sheriff Harland." Jacob held her gaze for a long moment. "You will stay here until I return, *ja*?"

The statement was more of an order than a question, but she let it slide. "*Ja*, I will wait here."

"Sehr gut." The relief in his expression was obvious. She couldn't help but watch as he walked away.

"Ms. Miller? Are you ready to start?" Jacy asked.

"Rachel, please." She managed a weak smile. "And yes. I'm ready."

The process was more difficult than she'd imagined. So many questions about the shape of his head, his eyes, brows, nose and mouth. Rachel knew she was failing miserably as a witness.

"I'm sorry, I just don't remember," she said for what felt like the hundredth time. "I wish I could be more specific."

Jacy smiled, nodded, then flipped a page of her sketch book. "What about this man?"

Rachel gasped. "Yes! That is him!" She stared at the image in shock. There was something about his eyes that nagged at her. But she shook off the sensation. She did not know this man; of that much she was certain sure. "How did you know?"

"Jacob helped create this sketch." Jacy tilted her head to the side. "Can you think of anything to fix? Anything that doesn't mesh with what you remember?"

Her mind went back to those harrowing moments when the gunman put the hood over her head, his hard fingers digging into her arms. The way he'd dragged her toward the car. He'd smelled like tobacco, but that wasn't much help when creating his likeness on the paper.

"I'm sorry, but I can't think of anything else." Rachel felt like a failure. "Everything happened so fast, both times I saw him. Today he tried to kidnap me but put a hood over my head, making it impossible to see his face. I can say with certainty that Jacob's sketch is exactly how I remember him, too."

"Well, that's good. Honestly, it's a good thing you

don't have anything for me to change. You'd be surprised at how many times two witnesses see the same person very differently. It's a relief that's not the case here." Jacy's positive attitude was sweet, but Rachel knew the sketch artist had hoped for more.

"What else can we do to help?" Rachel asked.

"I know that Sheriff Harland has already provided this sketch to the deputies across all of Green Lake County, so I'm sure they will find him very soon."

"I pray that is so." Rachel clasped her hands together in her lap to stop them from shaking. It seemed odd that she was feeling so off balance, despite the way Jacob had rescued her. She summoned a smile. "*Denke* for your help, Jacy."

"My pleasure." Jacy stood. "It looks like Jacob is finished with Liam."

Rachel glanced over to see both men striding toward her. As usual, Jacob's expression was grim; the man rarely smiled. Not that he had much to smile about after the events that had transpired today.

Her fault, for being so stubborn.

"Liam." Jacy handed the sheriff the sketch Jacob had done. "This is the man your deputies should be searching for."

Liam nodded, although Rachel could tell he seemed confused that it was the same one he already had.

"I wasn't much help, I'm afraid," Rachel said. "Jacob did a fine job, *ain't so*?"

"It's good," Liam admitted. Then he came over to take the seat Jacy had recently vacated. Setting the sketch aside, he met her gaze. "How are you holding up?"

"Sehr gut," she answered automatically.

"Jacob told me about how the gunman tried to get you into the back of his vehicle. He threw a hood over your head and tried to pull you inside, correct?"

"*Ja*, that is true." She thought back, knowing those moments would be etched in her mind for a long time. "He was driving a white car this time, not a dark blue truck. And there were two men, a driver and the man who grabbed me."

Liam's gaze was compassionate. "I'm sure that was very scary. Think back, Rachel. Is there anything else you can tell me about what happened?"

"I was throwing the garbage into the dumpster when I saw the car." She hesitated, thinking back. "I believe it must have been parked there, waiting for me."

"Go on," Liam urged.

"The door opened, and that's when the man tossed the hood over my head and began to drag me into the car. He smelled like tobacco." She frowned, wishing she'd reacted to the threat sooner. "I believe he was the gunman, too."

"He was." Jacob spoke with confidence. "And the white car was used rather than the blue truck to throw us off guard."

She nodded. If she'd seen the blue truck, she wouldn't have bothered with the garbage. "*Ja*, that is what I think, too."

"You didn't catch a license plate number?" Liam asked.

Rachel shook her head. "I still had the hood on when I heard the car drive away."

"I was too focused on Rachel to take note of the plate number." Jacob sounded frustrated with himself.

"Things happened fast. Once I grasped Rachel's arm, the man threw her toward me with such force I was knocked off balance. Before I could regain my footing, he'd jumped back inside the car. The driver instantly took off."

Liam thought about this for a moment. "Did either of you see a gun? Or a knife?"

"I did not," Jacob admitted. "But I recognized the gunman certain sure."

The man's eyes flashed in her mind. What was it about them that bothered her? She told herself that it was that terrible moment he'd shouted at them to pull the buggy over or he would shoot. She shivered. Never before had she been grabbed by a man intent on hurting her.

Her usual confidence was sorely shaken.

Liam nodded, then slowly rose. "Okay, I appreciate you coming in to help with the sketch."

"I didn't do anything," she murmured. "The details were all provided by Jacob."

Jacob rested a hand on her shoulder. "Rachel has been through a lot today. It's understandable she doesn't remember everything as clearly as you would like. I hope you find this man soon, Liam."

"Me, too." Liam sighed. "Rachel, I need you to keep the café closed for a few days."

"*Ja*, I understand." It pained her to lose several days of work, but the recent kidnapping attempt made it clear the gunman would return to find her there.

As much as she hated to admit it, Jacob had been right. She never should have gone to work today. It was clear she would be safer at home, within her Amish community. Mayhap this was God's way of reminding her of her roots.

"Glad to hear it." Liam sounded satisfied. "Every deputy on staff will continue to keep an eye on the place, in case the white car or the blue truck return. Are you ready? It's time I drive you home."

Jacob stepped back, giving her room to stand. She followed the men through the maze of desks, grateful to note Liam was heading out the same side door she'd used yesterday.

Liam and Jacob kept her between them as they crossed the parking lot to an SUV that was not marked as a police vehicle. She was secretly relieved she and Jacob wouldn't be returning to their community in a police car. Some of the Amish had softened a bit toward Liam after the events that had unfolded at Christmas, but she also knew the elders, like Ezekiel Moore and Bishop Bachman, would want to know why the sheriff was involved.

She hated the idea of bringing danger to their community.

Jacob sat in the front seat alongside Liam, leaving her to take the back. As Liam headed toward her home, she bowed her head and prayed for strength and guidance.

Her heart ached with fear and worry over the idea that closing her café for good was part of God's plan for her.

Jacob hoped that Rachel wouldn't change her mind again over closing her café for a few days. He tried to relax his tense muscles, reminding himself that barking orders wasn't the way to convince Rachel to do the right thing.

Although he did not understand why she acted so stubborn.

He considered going to the elders and Bishop Bachman to request their guidance with Rachel. Surely, she would listen to their counsel.

Although, he couldn't help but wonder why they'd allowed her to open the café downtown in the first place. If she was his wife, he would not allow it.

The thought quickly made him backpedal in his mind. Rachel would never be his wife. He wasn't interested in being married again.

And even if he was, she would not be high on his list of potential suitors. The woman was too independent. Too maddening.

"Shall I drop you both off at your place, Jacob?"

He glanced at Liam and nodded. "*Ja*, that would be *sehr gut. Denke.*"

"Please, Liam, I would ask that you drop me off at home, first," Rachel spoke up. "It is not proper for me to be at Jacob's farm."

Jacob swallowed a sigh of frustration. Normally he held himself to the strict Amish ways, but his fear over Rachel's well-being was more compelling than his need for structure. "I understand you do not wish to stay, but I was hoping you would consider making dinner again, as we have not eaten."

"*Ach*, of course. I will be happy to prepare a meal." Rachel agreed so quickly, he felt a bit guilty for playing on her kindness.

Secretly, he was relieved she'd agreed, as Rachel was an excellent cook.

The radio on Liam's collar squawked. "Sheriff? This is Marie in dispatch. Will you please provide your current location?"

Liam reached up to press the button. "Heading down the highway toward the Amish community, why?"

"We have a report about a dead body being found along the south side of Green Lake," the dispatcher continued. "Body is that of a male in his midfifties. The ME's office is on the way to help get him out of the water, but they would like you to get there as soon as possible."

A dead body? A male in his midfifties? Jacob wondered if it was the same man Rachel had seen stabbed in the alley behind her café.

"Ten-four, I'll head over." Liam released the radio, then glanced at Rachel using the rearview mirror. "Rachel, I hate to ask this of you, but I'd like to take you and Jacob with me to the crime scene."

"You think it's the same man I saw lurking outside the café? The one who was stabbed?" she asked fearfully.

"Maybe, maybe not." Liam shrugged. "We won't know for sure until we see the body up close."

"No, Liam. Rachel does not need to see a dead man," Jacob said firmly. "She has been traumatized enough for one day. I must insist you take us home."

Liam didn't answer, his gaze going back to the rearview mirror. Finally he said, "It's true this is not the usual protocol, but I'll waste valuable time driving back and forth for Rachel to assist in identifying him. It would be easier if we could go together."

"Easier for you, not for Rachel," Jacob insisted.

"I will speak for myself, Jacob," Rachel said in a soft voice. "While I do not wish to view a dead man, it seems reasonable for Liam to request my help in identifying the man who was stabbed, *ain't so*? Mayhap this will help to find the killer."

He clenched his jaw so tight he was shocked he didn't crack a tooth. "Why must you see it now? Certain sure Liam could bring a picture by later."

"I could do that," Liam agreed. His expression was pained as he added, "It's your choice, Rachel. I will honor your wishes."

There was a long silence before she responded, "We should go now. I would rather have this unpleasant task finished sooner than later, *ja*?"

Jacob wondered if Rachel disobeyed his wishes on purpose, just to vex him. To his credit, Liam didn't immediately turn around. He waited for Jacob to agree.

"Fine." It was not easy to hide his frustration. He was only trying to do what was in Rachel's best interests. Seeing a dead man in person would be far more upsetting than seeing a photograph.

"I would be willing to stop somewhere on the way home to grab you both something to eat," Liam offered. He stopped the car and made a turn in the road to drive in the direction they'd just come from. The Amish community was west of the downtown area of Green Lake.

"No need to trouble yourself, Liam. I don't mind cooking for Jacob."

His frustration eased a bit at her words. Mayhap he

was wrong to have suggested she wait. As she'd mentioned, she preferred to get this task finished so she could move on with the rest of her evening.

"*Denke*, Rachel." He cleared his throat, doing his best to let go of his ire. "I hope this does not take too long, Liam."

"I'll do my best to get you back very soon."

A long silence filled the interior of the vehicle as Liam drove to the south shore of the lake. As Liam pulled over to the side of the road, Jacob could see a small gathering of people huddled around something lying on the ground.

A body, covered with a cloth, thankfully.

He hated the idea of taking Rachel over to see the dead man, but resolutely pushed open his door. If she insisted on doing this, he would accompany her.

"Give me a minute," Liam said. The sheriff quickened his pace to join the group. From where he and Rachel stood, Jacob watched Liam kneel beside the body and lift the edge of the cloth. He spoke to the men around him, then nodded and rose to his feet.

"Rachel? Jacob?" Liam waved them over.

The ground was uneven here, so Jacob rested his hand on Rachel's elbow, guiding her. As they approached, a knot of dread formed in his belly.

Rachel didn't look happy to be in this situation, either, but she didn't hesitate. When they reached the body, Liam lifted the sheet.

The dead man did not look familiar to him, but Rachel gasped and nodded. "That's the man who was stabbed in the alley," she whispered. Then she turned and hid her face against his shirt.

This was exactly what he'd wanted to spare her, but he couldn't help wrapping his arms around her in a reassuring hug.

A sense of foreboding wouldn't leave him alone. Rachel was in danger, now more than ever.

And for the first time in a long time, he prayed that God might keep Rachel safe within their Amish community.

FIVE

Biting her lip to prevent a cry, Rachel leaned against Jacob, grateful for his support. Even with her eyes closed, the dead man's face was seared in her mind. Why had he spent two days lingering outside her café? What had he and the man in the blue truck talked about in the alley? Why had he been stabbed?

What was going on?

"Rachel?" Jacob's low voice rumbled near her ear. "Are you all right?"

No one would be okay after seeing a dead man. Yet it had been her decision to come here to identify him, so she forced herself to nod. After another moment, she lifted her head and stepped back. "*Denke*, Jacob. I will be fine now."

He did not look convinced. She felt certain her distress was written on her features. Yet she was still glad she had come to get this over with. She had done her duty. The rest was up to Liam and his Green Lake County deputies.

"Liam? I would ask that you please take us home." Jacob's tone was firm. He slipped a hand beneath her elbow. "We are ready to leave."

"Yes, of course." Liam didn't protest. He covered the man's face and stepped away from the body. "I appreciate you doing this, Rachel."

"I hope it helps you find the man who killed him," she said softly.

"I hope so, too." Liam sounded grim and she knew he was troubled by the way violence had returned to Green Lake. Normally this was a beautiful and peaceful area. According to her mother, that serenity had been one of the reasons many of the Amish had moved here so many years ago.

Their community had experienced a modest growth over the years. A small family of Amish had recently joined them from Minnesota, while another family had come from Illinois. On the other hand, there were always some who chose to leave their community to experience life within the *Englisch* world.

Was Bishop Bachman right to ask her to find a suitor? Was this God's way of telling her she needed to find someone to marry, sooner than later? Her gaze darted to Jacob walking tall beside her. His expression could have been carved in stone, and she knew he was still angry with her over this small detour.

No, she was not interested in Jacob, a man very set in his ways. She knew without being told he would not want his wife to work at a café in town.

Yet it was sweet that he'd gone out of his way to comfort her. It was reassuring to discover he had a heart buried somewhere beneath that grumpy exterior.

Liam unlocked the SUV. Jacob opened the back passenger door for her. Minutes later, they were back on the road heading for home.

Rachel tried not to think about the dead man. Or the man who'd tried to kidnap her. She tried to focus her attention on making Jacob a meal.

Not that she was the least bit hungry. Identifying the dead man had ruined her appetite. Yet, Jacob had done much for her over the past twenty-four hours, so the least she could do was repay him with a home-cooked meal.

"Rachel? Your house or Jacob's?" Liam asked.

"Mine," Jacob said before she could respond. "It's closer than Rachel's, and I will walk her home later."

Liam's gaze held hers in the rearview mirror. She nodded. "Jacob's home is fine, Liam. I will make our evening meal while he cares for the livestock, *ja*?"

"Sounds good," Liam agreed.

"You are welcome to stay," she offered.

Liam shook his head. "Thanks, but Shauna is waiting for me. We try to eat dinner together each night."

It was a nice tradition, possibly carried over from Liam's time with the Amish. She remembered David mentioning how his niece Shauna, who was married to Liam, had recently finished her college degree. A formal education like that was not valued by the Amish. They preferred the simple life, learning life skills like farming, cooking and carpentry.

"I'm sure Shauna enjoys spending time with you, Liam."

"It's my favorite part of the day," he admitted with a grin.

Jacob remained silent until Liam pulled into the driveway of his home. Then he said, "*Denke* for the ride, Liam."

"You're welcome."

"Enjoy your dinner." Rachel climbed out of the vehicle and stood beside Jacob as Liam drove away.

"Komm." Jacob led the way inside the house, then stood awkwardly for a moment, as if unsure what to say.

"*Ach*, dinner will be ready shortly." She brushed past him to the kitchen.

"I'll return once I've cared for the livestock," Jacob said with a nod.

Rachel managed to pull a simple meal together but made a mental note of items Jacob would need to obtain for future meals. There wasn't time to make more bread, so she made do with leftovers.

Jacob returned from the barn, removing his hat then crossing over to wash up in the sink. She was struck again by how handsome he was. Even more so, she thought with a sigh, if he would smile.

"The meal looks and smells *sehr gut*." He took the same chair as he had last evening.

"Denke." She reached over to take his hand. "You'll say grace?"

He bowed his head. "Dear Lord, we thank You for this food You have provided to us. We also thank You for keeping Rachel safe in Your care, amen."

"Amen." She held his hand a moment longer before releasing him. "I will make the most of my few days off work," she said as they began to eat. "If we do not stock up on supplies, it will be difficult to make meals moving forward, certain sure."

Jacob met her gaze for a moment, then turned his attention back to his meal. "I don't expect you to continue cooking for me."

"I know, but I don't mind helping." She took a bite of her roast beef, her appetite returning. "I hope the animals didn't suffer while you were in town today?"

"No, they are fine." He frowned. "But I'm very glad you are not going to the café tomorrow. We must give Liam and his deputies time to catch this murderer."

"Ja." She hoped and prayed for the terrible man to be arrested very soon.

When they finished eating, she began cleaning up. Jacob headed back outside to bring in wood for the stove.

"Well then." She smoothed her hands over her apron. "I need to return home."

Jacob frowned. "I do not like you staying there alone."

She lifted a brow. "You know I must. We do not have a chaperone, and truly, I will be fine. All the attacks against me have taken place in town. I am certain sure the killer will not find me here."

He held her gaze for a long moment. "I hope you are right about that."

She hoped so, too.

Jacob turned, retrieved his hat and opened the door. She donned her cloak and headed outside.

As they walked down his driveway to the road, she realized this was the second time they had walked like this, together. If others noticed, it would be assumed they were courting.

She glanced around, hoping no one was out and about to see them.

"What is it?" Jacob frowned, looking around the area. "Do you see something?"

"No, but the more time we spend together, the more likely tongues will begin to wag."

"Bah." Jacob waved a dismissive hand. "Our friendship is not anyone's business."

"Friendship?" She couldn't help teasing him a bit. "Are we friends, Jacob?"

His scowl deepened, which ironically made her want to laugh. "Acquaintances, then."

"*Ach*, Jacob, certain sure we are more than acquaintances," she chided. "We have shared several meals together. And even more importantly, we are helping each other out, *ain't so*?"

He sighed. "What do you want from me, Rachel? I said we are friends."

"I was surprised to hear you say that." Oddly, the grim task she'd done earlier seemed to fade away when she was teasing Jacob. "And I like being your friend."

A flash of surprise darkened his eyes, but he didn't say anything more. She had the impression that he'd spoken without thinking, and only now realized what he'd admitted.

He halted at her front door. "Do you need more wood for the stove?"

"I don't think so." She opened the door and stepped inside. There was a chill in the air, but she knew it wouldn't take long for the wood-burning stove to warm the place.

Jacob followed her in. He lit the woodstove, then stood. "I'm not far if you need something."

"*Denke*, but I will be fine." She hoped the more she said those words, the more she would find a way to believe them. "I will see you tomorrow, Jacob."

He looked confused for a moment, as if not understanding why she would see him, but simply nodded. "Sleep well, Rachel."

"Good night." She followed him to the door, closing it behind him.

The moment Jacob was gone, she shivered. Not because the room still held a chill, but because she hadn't realized how difficult it would be to stay alone.

The image of the dead man's face flashed in her mind. She ruthlessly pushed it away. The man was in God's hands. And so was she. There was no reason to be afraid.

Rachel forced herself to turn and walk to her room, desperately trying to ignore the urge to run after Jacob to beg him to stay.

Jacob stood outside Rachel's house for several minutes, unable to simply walk away. Should he stick around for a while? The temperature was still cool for mid-May, but at least it wasn't raining.

The situation was troubling, and one that he really wasn't sure how to handle. Rachel's comment about others noticing them walking together had struck home. Couples who were courting walked together often. He knew that anyone watching them together would assume the same. It would not take long for the news to reach Bishop Bachman, who would want to make it official.

The mere thought of courting Rachel bothered him. He'd lost his wife and son. And was not interested in replacing them.

Not now, not ever.

The stern resolve spurred him into action. He turned

and walked away from Rachel's house, before he could do something foolish.

There were many Amish homes in the area. The attacker would have no way of finding her here. Besides, he'd agreed to help protect Rachel by providing buggy rides to and from the café. Now that she'd agreed to stay home, his services were no longer needed.

He needed to think about his farm, and the upcoming planting. His livestock were doing well, but he needed to reinforce the chicken coop to protect against foxes and other wildlife.

There were reports among the elders about mountain lions being seen nearby. He'd need to keep a sharp eye out for predators that threatened his livelihood. He reminded himself to bring his rifle with him while working in the barn and driving the buggy.

Jacob had buried himself in his work after losing Anna and Isaac. He would do that again now. To distract him from Rachel.

He froze at the sound of a car engine. The vehicle was approaching from the direction of downtown Green Lake. Jacob instinctively moved toward the closest tree, hoping his dark clothing would help provide cover.

From his position behind the large oak tree, he watched the vehicle approach. It was a white sedan and it was moving slowly down the highway. Normally, he appreciated when cars drove slowly through their Amish community, hopefully to avoid causing a buggy accident.

But it was a white car exactly like the one used in the attempt to kidnap Rachel.

A coincidence? White cars were common enough, he supposed, but not necessarily here.

He didn't move, barely took a breath as the white sedan rolled past. Staring at the back of the car, he tried to make out the license plate.

But he couldn't see any letters or numbers. There was nothing but a dark smear where they should have been. The outside of the license plate could be seen, but nothing more. Had the driver covered the plate in mud? If so, that only made him more suspicious that the driver was the same one who'd tried to kidnap Rachel.

He needed to call Liam. But he did not have a phone, and Rachel didn't, either.

But David McKay did. The elders had agreed to let him use it for business purposes. David made furniture by hand that he sold at the Amish Shoppe. He did beautiful work, as did his wife, Elizabeth, who made quilts. Together they shared one phone.

David and Elizabeth were his neighbors and they'd helped each other out over the past few months. He was about to head that way when he paused, second-guessing himself.

Was it necessary to do this tonight? Liam had mentioned having dinner with his wife. Calling now, especially after the car was gone, wouldn't help. Not when he hadn't been able to get a license plate number.

No, there was no reason to intrude on David and Elizabeth, or Liam and Shauna. Mayhap he would have a chance to talk to them in the morning. Since Liam was married to Shauna, David's niece, he knew they saw each other often. He felt certain David would find a way to get a message to Liam.

He was about to step away from the tree to head toward his home when he saw another car approaching from the opposite direction. With a dark scowl, he moved closer to the tree, watching the vehicle. What if it headed toward Rachel's house?

It didn't. After the car drove past, he realized not only was it not white in color, but the driver was going fast. Too much so to be looking for someone.

Feeling foolish for overreacting, Jacob abruptly turned and strode home. He didn't like the idea of Rachel being in danger, and would protect her as necessary, but this was not his mystery to solve.

An *Englisch* man had died, and it was the *Englisch* law enforcement who would find the person responsible and bring him to justice.

Entering his home, the loneliness hit him like a fist to the stomach. So different than when Rachel had been there. He'd appreciated her cooking while he finished his chores.

Enough. He preferred being alone. He fed wood into the fire, then retreated to his room.

Yet despite everything that had happened, sleep did not come easily. His muscles were tired, but his mind raced. The white car, the dead man, the near kidnapping.

Rachel stepping into his arms. Holding on to him for support.

He tossed and turned, slept in fits and starts. By five o'clock in the morning, he gave up and donned his work clothes. He stoked the fire, then made coffee.

Dawn was already brightening the sky by the time he headed to the barn. There was a chill in the air, but the sun held a promise of nicer weather to come. A good sign that he would be able to begin planting next week as planned.

His lack of sleep did not intrude on his ability to fall into the easy rhythm of his routine chores. Yet he kept an eye out for signs of David moving about outside. The McKays did not have a barn full of livestock or farmland the way he did, but they had added a cow for fresh milk, and a few chickens. David's barn had been destroyed by a fire back in December, and the Amish community was coming together after the spring planting to help him rebuild.

The Amish took care of their own.

That thought took him right back to Rachel. Certain sure that was why he'd struggled to rest last night. He'd been trying to push concerns for her welfare from his mind, but he could not.

In fact, just the opposite. He should let the Amish elders and Bishop Bachman know about the danger she was in.

He was just finishing his chores when he saw David and Elizabeth step outside. They were obviously on their way to the Amish Shoppe, where they sold their handmade goods.

"David! Elizabeth!" Jacob held up his hand and hurried toward them. "May I have a moment?"

"Of course, Jacob." David smiled broadly, and there was no doubt he and Elizabeth were extremely happy together. "What can we do for you?"

"I would like you to keep an eye out for a white sedan. I saw one driving very slowly through our community last night, and I am afraid there are *Englischers* seeking to cause trouble for Rachel."

"For Rachel?" Elizabeth echoed. "Why would she be in danger?"

He took a moment to fill them in on the attempted kidnapping, and the dead man who had been pulled from Green Lake. David's expression was grim, and Jacob knew his neighbor was remembering a time six months ago when he and Elizabeth had been in danger, too.

"You say the license plate was covered in some way?" David asked.

"Yes." He grimaced. "I helped Liam with a sketch of the man who tried to kidnap Rachel, but I don't have his likeness with me."

"I will ask Liam to show the drawing to all of us working within the Amish Shoppe," David said. "If Rachel is in danger, then the entire Amish community must remain on high alert for this man."

It was a good idea and one Jacob hadn't considered. "I have not spoken to the elders or bishop about this yet, but I hope to do that soon." Jacob already felt better knowing David and Elizabeth would reach out to Liam.

"Rachel is at her house, alone?" Elizabeth frowned. "I don't like that. She's vulnerable there."

"If the white car returns, I will ask about having someone else stay with her." Jacob turned to glance down the road to Rachel's house. "I'm heading there now to check on her."

"Sehr gut," Elizabeth said, putting a hand on his arm. "You are a good neighbor, Jacob."

He felt himself flush, knowing that while he might

be a good neighbor now, he hadn't always been. "Please let me know if Liam has any updates on this case. In the meantime, Rachel is keeping her café closed."

"*Ach*, that must be difficult for her," Elizabeth said. "Please let her know I'm thinking of her and can help in any way."

"We must go, but we will keep in touch," David said.

He nodded. "Have a good day." Turning away, he went to fetch one of the long-dead trees he'd decided to give to Rachel. Once he'd lugged it to her house, he picked up the axe and went to work.

"Jacob? What are you doing here?" Rachel appeared in the doorway, looking beautiful as always.

Before he could answer, a familiar black SUV pulled up. He set down the axe when he saw Liam emerge from the car.

"Did you find him?" Jacob asked, hoping and praying Rachel's nightmare would be over.

"Jacob, Rachel." Liam shook his head. "I'm afraid I'm not coming with good news."

Jacob instinctively moved closer to Rachel. "Bad news, then."

Liam sighed. "Yes. Rachel's Café has been vandalized. Someone broke the front window to get inside. I don't think there's been a lot of other damage, but Rachel is the only one who would know for sure if anything is missing or broken."

Jacob imagined the driver of the white car breaking into the café out of anger over his inability to find Rachel.

He shivered, hating the idea of Rachel being in danger from someone who would not hesitate to harm her.

SIX

"I need to see the damaged café." Tears pricked at Rachel's eyes, but she refused to succumb. Lifting her chin, she met Liam's gaze. "Today. After we break our fast."

"There's no reason to go. Seeing it will not change the outcome," Jacob protested.

She turned to stare at him. "There is a reason. I need to see what has been damaged so I can repair and replace the items."

Jacob scowled and looked as if he would continue to argue. Liam held up a hand as if calling a truce. "I'm sorry but I'm not able to take you there until later. I just stopped by to let you know about the damage."

"*Denke*, Liam." She knew the sheriff had gone out of his way to inform her of the incident. He could have had one of his deputies do the notification, but Liam's ties to the Amish community had compelled him to come to deliver the news personally.

"As long as you are here, Liam," Jacob said, "I should tell you that last night, I saw a white car drive past Rachel's house. The vehicle moved very slowly, and while I'm no expert on cars, it appeared to be the same make and model of the one used in the attempted kidnapping."

"What time?" Liam asked, his eyes bright with interest.

"Roughly quarter to nine—dusk had already fallen. I hid by the tree, so he would not see me. Unfortunately, I could not get a license plate number." Jacob frowned. "The plate seemed covered in some way."

Rachel was surprised by the news. "You did not tell me this, Jacob."

"I intended to do so today." Jacob turned toward Liam. "I mentioned the incident to David and Elizabeth. They were planning to get in touch with you."

"That's good to know, but I am concerned about the license plate being covered," Liam admitted. "I've seen mud used to cover license plates—that could be what was done in this case. It seems the driver had done it on purpose, which is very suspicious."

"My thought, as well." Jacob tugged on the brim of his hat. "I also believe that the driver's frustration with not finding Rachel caused him to vandalize her café."

Liam considered this. "Maybe, that is one consideration. But a more likely scenario is that the killer thought she might be staying in the small apartment over the café. When he didn't find her there, he drove around looking for her."

"An apartment above the café?" Jacob's eyes widened in surprise. He swung to face her. "You never mentioned there was a room up there."

"I mostly use it for storage." She didn't add how often she'd considered giving her house to an Amish family in need, and moving up to the apartment for good.

The only thing that had prevented her from making the move was being isolated from her community. She did not want to take after her father, who had abruptly left his Amish life, wife and daughter behind.

She didn't have a family to abandon, the way he had. But she did not want to leave her Amish roots, either. She still remembered Bishop Bachman's concern about her café being in town, and possibly subject to *Englisch* influence.

"I need to get back to town," Liam quickly spoke up. She imagined he didn't want to be dragged into an argument between them.

And really, why did everything with Jacob need to be an argument? Why was it her fault he hadn't known about the apartment above the café?

"I will return in a few hours to take you to the café," Liam called as he strode toward his SUV.

Jacob's cheeks flushed and he looked even more disgruntled than ever. For a long moment neither spoke, until Jacob said, "You should have told me about the apartment, *ain't so*?"

"Mayhap, but it simply didn't occur to me." She sighed and turned away. "I will begin making eggs so we can break our fast. You are welcome to join me, Jacob."

Without waiting for his response, she hurried back inside the house.

Through the window, she watched him remove his hat, run his fingers through his hair as if tempted to rip them out by the roots before plopping his hat back on his head. Frustration was etched on his features.

Shaking her head, she went to the kitchen. As she prepared the early-morning meal, she couldn't help thinking more about the enigmatic Jacob instead of her recently vandalized café. If the man would simply accept that he couldn't control everything and everyone, he would be much happier.

God was in control, not man.

Outside Jacob resumed chopping wood for her. She was grateful he'd taken on that chore as it was not her favorite. A necessity, of course. But soon, summer would be upon them, so the wood would only be needed for cooking.

Not heating.

By the time she'd finished making their meal, Jacob had come inside the house, taking his hat off and setting it on a chair. "You should be set for the next week," he announced.

"*Denke*, Jacob. That was very kind of you." She gestured to the table. "*Komm*, have a seat."

Jacob did, his eyes wide with appreciation as he saw the food. "This is *sehr gut*, Rachel."

She inclined her head, dishing out eggs, fresh bread and jam. She sat beside him, and bowed her head, waiting for him to say grace.

"Lord, we thank You for this food and for continuing to keep Rachel safe in Your care, amen."

"Amen." She thought he sounded more comfortable today, compared to the first time she'd asked him to say grace.

They ate in silence for a few moments. She was about to ask about the white car when Jacob abruptly spoke.

"You need to close the café."

She blinked, then frowned. "It has been closed." Then understanding dawned. "*Ach*, you mean I should shut down my business permanently."

"Ja." He stared at her. "It's too far from the community. Certain sure you could find another place close by."

Anger flashed. Somehow, she managed to keep her tone even. "I need to be where the customers are, *ain't so*? And I don't recall asking for your opinion, Jacob Strauss. The elders have given their blessing—that's what matters."

His frown deepened. "Mayhap their opinion will change once they hear of the danger you've experienced. The threat from the *Englischers*."

"You would attempt to sway them?" She set her fork down and clasped her hands beneath the table. "Against my wishes?"

He looked away, then sighed heavily. "No, I will not do that against your wishes. However, you must be the one to tell them the truth, Rachel. As a member of the community it is your duty."

She grimaced, hating to admit he was right. But at least he wouldn't rush over to the elders as soon as they'd finished their meal. Her hope was that it would not take long for Liam and his deputies to find the man responsible. Once the danger was over, she would happily explain what had happened.

When they finished eating, Jacob brought in the recently chopped wood, stacking it near the stove as she cleaned up. She'd begun making more bread and at one point he came to peer over her shoulder.

"Smells delicious."

"Denke." She hoped it was the heat of cooking that made her feel flushed, not a silly reaction to Jacob's appreciation.

Once he was finished with the wood, he stood by the door. "I need to repair my chicken coop. But I would like to accompany you to the café, if you insist on going."

"That is fine with me. I will be along shortly, once I've finished with the bread."

He nodded, then left. When she finished with the bread, she pulled jam, pickled beets and other items to take over with the bread.

The walk wasn't far, but she found herself glancing warily over her shoulder for the white car.

After she put the items away in Jacob's kitchen, she saw Liam pull up the driveway. Jacob walked over from the chicken coop, greeting him with a nod.

"Ready to go?" Liam asked.

"*Ja*, we appreciate the ride, Liam," she said with a smile.

Ten minutes later Liam pulled up in front of the café. She eyed the broken window, feeling dejected. Things could be replaced, but it would cost time and money.

Inside, she poked around to see what, if anything, might be missing. Aside from the broken glass, everything else looked intact. Things were moved, though, as if someone had been searching for something.

No, not a thing, but a person. She shivered as she understood Liam's theory to be correct. The killer had come here to find her.

And there was no doubt in her mind he would be back.

Watching Rachel straighten her café was difficult. As much as he wished she'd close her business for good—

had in fact ordered her to do such a thing—he did not like seeing her so upset.

She worked hard, shared her skill in the kitchen with those who appreciated a good Amish meal. Certain sure she didn't deserve this.

He'd known telling her to close was a mistake. Yet he also couldn't understand why she was being so stubborn. As she moved around in the kitchen, he climbed the stairs to the apartment that he hadn't realized was up there. As she'd mentioned, there were boxes along with a tired-looking sofa and chair. He was surprised to see there was a small kitchen area, too.

The dust on several surfaces was disturbed, proof the intruder had come up here searching for Rachel. It made his blood run cold at the thought of him mounting the stairs with his gun, hoping to find her alone and vulnerable.

How long before he tracked her to her home within their community?

Not long, he thought grimly.

After returning to the main level, he searched for something to cover the broken glass.

"I have some leftover wood and other supplies in the basement," Rachel said.

"Okay." As promised, he found several different sizes of plywood. Ten minutes later, he'd nailed a section of plywood over the broken glass.

"Is anything missing?" Liam asked.

Rachel shook her head. "No, just moved around. Only the glass was broken, certain sure to gain access to the café."

"The intruder went upstairs, clearly hoping to find

Rachel." Jacob frowned. "Although I don't know how he knew it was there."

"I wondered about that, too," Liam admitted. "From the outside you can see there are windows on a second floor, but why would he think to find Rachel there?"

"I've stayed up there on occasion," Rachel said.

Jacob lifted a brow. "When? And why?"

"Mostly during inclement weather." She shrugged. "I don't like it, but it's better than walking in a blizzard or a tornado, *ja*?"

"The tornado sirens went off last Friday," Liam said. "Did you stay here that night?"

"I did." Her eyes widened. "*Ach*, you think this man has been watching me since then?"

It irked him that he hadn't known about Rachel spending the night up in the apartment during bad weather. And as recently as five nights ago.

"Yes, I do," Liam said. His radio squawked and he turned away. After a moment he said, "Okay, thanks, Garrett."

"Did he find something?" Jacob asked.

"A white car, but it's not the one we've been looking for. It belongs to a married couple from Chicago, Illinois."

Jacob wasn't familiar with the other cities and states in the area, mostly because he was a simple farmer and didn't interact much with the *Englisch*. He raised livestock and crops that were used within the community.

Rachel must have sensed his confusion. "Many people come from the Chicago area to visit. And we're looking for two men, not a married couple."

"Is it your plan to pull over and question everyone

driving a white car?" Jacob arched a brow as he regarded Liam. "It would be easy enough as this is not yet the height of the tourist season."

"We have specifically been searching for a white car with muddy or covered plates," Liam said. "But yes, we are also running the plates of other white vehicles, too. The one from Chicago piqued our interest because they were from out of state."

"What makes you believe someone from outside Wisconsin wants to kidnap me?" Rachel asked.

Liam shrugged. "We have learned the identity of the dead man." The sheriff turned to Rachel. "Does the name Greg Sharma mean anything to you?"

"Greg Sharma?" Rachel repeated. "No, I have never heard the name Greg Sharma."

"Turns out that our victim, who died of his abdominal stab wound as you said, Rachel, is from Chicago." Liam grimaced. "That's why the white car with Illinois plates caught my deputy's attention. He asked them several questions and ran their names through the database, but the man and woman did not have any criminal records, so we obviously let them go."

"Chicago is known for crime?" Jacob asked.

"They are, but so are many other places nearby. I hate to say it, but crime is everywhere, even here in Green Lake."

Jacob knew that to be true. It was one of the reasons the Amish preferred to stay among themselves. "It doesn't make sense regardless of where the criminal has come from," he felt compelled to point out. "There's no rational reason why anyone would kidnap an Amish woman."

"I did witness a murder," Rachel murmured.

"*Ja*, but why go through the trouble to kidnap you?" He remembered how the man in the blue truck had told him to pull over or he'd shoot, when he so easily could have fired his gun twice, killing them both while still having time to drive away without being caught. "It would seem simpler to eliminate you as a threat, rather than pushing you into a car."

"Trust me, we're looking at all angles," Liam said with a sigh. "The dead man is a place to start. We're working with the Chicago police to get more information on Sharma."

The way Liam spoke about the investigation made him realize they were not likely to get this man into custody anytime soon. No reason to stick around here any longer than necessary.

"We would be grateful for a ride back home," Jacob told Liam.

"Of course." Liam glanced at Rachel. "Is there anything else you need to do here?"

"No, as I said, nothing is damaged other than the window in the front door." She twisted her hands together for a moment, then sensing his gaze, dropped them to her sides. "I'm ready to go."

Liam's radio sounded again and he moved away once more to have a conversation. Jacob stepped closer to Rachel. "I don't think you should stay home alone."

"Jacob, we've had this discussion." She sounded tired. "The killer doesn't know where I live."

Not yet, he thought grimly. "But if he does find you, being alone makes you an easy target."

"*Ach*, you are so stubborn!" She threw up her hands

in defeat. "To do that we would need to find a chaperone to stay at your home, and that would mean telling others within the community about the danger, something reserved for the elders, *ain't so*?"

"*Ja*, but what about Leah Moore?" He'd noticed Leah, Rachel and Elizabeth usually sat together during the noon meal after services. "Mayhap she would not mind staying for a day or two."

Rachel slowly nodded. "She would, yes. Although she runs the Sunshine Café in the Amish Shoppe so she will not be available until evening. And her *grosspappi*, Ezekiel Moore, is one of the elders."

That was another reason he'd suggested Leah stay with them. He'd promised not to speak to the elders about the danger, as that was Rachel's duty. Perhaps Leah would convince Rachel to speak to them sooner rather than later.

"Thanks, Garrett." Liam finished with his call. "Let's go. I need to be out searching for the man in the sketch and the white car, too."

Rachel went back to the kitchen to make sure the back door was secure. Jacob hovered in the doorway waiting for her, but he needn't have worried. She didn't linger.

Outside, the spring temperature was warm. He hoped the sunshine was here to stay for a while. There was more work for him to do on the farm, but he held his impatience in check.

Liam appeared to be on high alert as he drove back toward Jacob's home. They were only a mile away when a familiar-looking vehicle came toward them from the opposite direction.

"Liam! See that dark blue truck?" Rachel's voice was urgent.

"Yes. Hang on." Liam hit the brakes, bringing the SUV to an abrupt stop just as the blue truck flew past them. Liam was forced to take a few minutes to turn around on the narrow highway before gunning the engine to follow.

"Garrett, I'm in pursuit of a dark blue truck," Liam spoke into his radio. "I'm on Highway TW, requesting backup."

Jacob silently prayed while gripping the armrest as Liam pushed the gas pedal to the floor, sending them flying down the highway.

Please, Lord, keep us safe in Your care!

SEVEN

Never in her life had she traveled so fast. Rachel noticed how hard Liam gripped the wheel as the SUV barreled down the road. The scenery went by in a blur, but she craned her neck, attempting to search the road ahead for the blue truck.

She didn't see it. After several minutes, Liam let up on the gas, slowing their pace.

"Where did it go?" Jacob asked.

"I don't know," Liam admitted. "I can't in good conscience keep driving at such a high rate of speed with you and Rachel in the car."

"I don't mind—certain sure it's important to find the driver of the truck, *ain't so*?" Rachel said, her voice shaky.

"Yes, but there's no sign of it." Liam gestured wearily to the road before them. "I lost too much time turning around. He was driving incredibly fast, so he must have noticed me before I recognized him. Maybe Garrett or one of my other deputies will see him as they approach from the other direction."

"I don't mind if we go a bit farther," Jacob said with a frown. "We may still find him."

But Liam shook his head. "I need to get you both home. Don't worry, my team will continue searching for the truck and the white car."

"Of course they will." She trusted Liam was doing his best. Yet, she could tell Jacob was disappointed as Liam turned the SUV around to head back to their Amish community. She understood his frustration. The police needed to find the person responsible for all of this so their lives could get back to normal.

God had sent them on this path for a reason, she reminded herself. It was not their place to question His will.

As Liam passed Jacob's house, he said, "Pull in here, Liam."

"No." She leaned forward in her seat. "Please drop me off at my home, Liam."

"What?" Jacob's sharp tone made her sigh with weariness. "You agreed to stay with me, remember?"

"*Ja*, I remember. But only with Leah as a chaperone and I have not spoken to her yet. Keep in mind, she will not be home until later this evening, after the Amish Shoppe has been closed for the day." When Jacob opened his mouth to argue, she added, "I have several things at my house that will need to be brought over, clothing and other things from my cellar to assist in cooking meals."

That gave him pause, as he clearly liked to eat. If not for her annoyance over his constant arguing, she'd have smiled. Mayhap the way to Jacob's heart was through his stomach.

Not that she wanted his heart, she hastily assured herself. No, she was not interested in Jacob in that way.

Mayhap he'd lightened up a bit over time, but he was still too somber and too set in his ways for her taste.

And she felt certain it was the same for him. She knew she vexed him, more often than not.

"Sehr gut," Jacob finally said. "But do not take too long to gather what you need. Certain sure the blue truck or white car could return at any moment, *ain't so*?"

"*Ja*, or mayhap the sheriff has scared him off for good." When Liam came to a stop, she pushed her door open. "*Denke*, Liam. I pray you find the killer soon."

"I'm praying for that, too," Liam agreed. "I want this man behind bars as much as you do."

With a nod, she stepped out of the vehicle, then closed the door behind her. Liam didn't immediately drive away, waiting until she walked up and into the house. Inside, she stood at the window and watched as Liam finally drove away, turning around to take Jacob home.

When they were gone, she headed into the kitchen. After looking around at what she had, she gathered items she'd need. She would bring as much as she could carry in her large basket. Certain sure Jacob didn't have much in the way of spices or pickled goods.

As she worked, she thought about Leah. She did not doubt that her friend would agree to stay with her and Jacob, although she would be surprised at the request. Jacob participated in services, but he did not mingle on a social level. His stern features did not welcome small talk.

She had to admit he'd softened some over the past two days. Just when she thought they could indeed be friends, as he'd mentioned, he reverted to barking out orders or finding a reason to argue.

After she had put everything together in her basket, including a nightgown and a change of clothing, she paused and glanced around the kitchen. After their hurried breakfast in the morning, she noticed there was a need to clean before heading out. She wanted her home to be ready for the moment she would be able to return.

She lost track of time as she worked, grateful to have tasks to focus on, rather than thinking about the damage to her café or the driver of the blue truck, who had likely gotten away.

And mayhap deep down, she wasn't quite ready to walk down the road to Jacob's. Not that she minded his company—he'd been nothing but polite, sweetly grateful for the meals she'd provided and protective of her safety. Yet spending time with him, even with a chaperone such as Leah, would create speculation among the community that they were courting.

Something she was certain sure Jacob did not want.

In truth she didn't want the idea to circulate around their friends and Amish family, either.

Yet Bishop Bachman's voice echoed in her head, reminding her of her duty to their community to marry and have a family. And she understood why that was so, even though she'd had no interest. There were several single men he'd suggested may be a good fit for her.

Jacob Strauss had not been one of them.

After drying her hands on her apron, she decided she could put it off no longer. When she heard a knock at her door, she froze, her mind instantly going to the man in the blue truck. Her gaze darted around the room, searching for a place to hide. The cellar? Yes, that would work.

The knock came again, and she frowned. Would a criminal knock? No, he would not. He would break in much the way he had to her café. Shaking her head at her foolishness, she hurried over to open the door.

"Mary!" She gaped in surprise to see Leah's mother, Mary Moore, standing there. "*Ach*, it's good to see you. *Wilkom*, what is it I can do for you?"

"*Denke*, Rachel." Mary smiled, moving slowly as she came inside. She remembered Leah mentioning her mother had some recent trouble with her hip. "Jacob stopped by to let me know you are in need of a chaperone."

He what? Why on earth would he do such a thing? It was all she could do not to snap. Instead, she forced a smile. "*Ach*, Mary, I'm sorry, but Jacob should not have approached you about this."

A frown furrowed Mary's brow. "He mentioned there was vandalism done to your café in town. He seems to believe you may be in danger. Is that not true?"

She drew in a deep breath, doing her best to remain calm. The reason she'd agreed to have Leah as a chaperone was that her friend would not assume there was something more going on between her and Jacob. It was possible Leah's mother, Mary, would have assumed such a thing anyway, but she was still annoyed. "It is true, vandalism has struck my café. The window in the door was broken, but that is all. Still, I don't believe there is danger here among our community."

Apart from the threat of her lashing out at Jacob. She could not believe he'd changed their arrangement without even speaking to her about it.

"*Ach*, well, I'm sure Jacob knows best, *ain't so*? I'm here, so we should continue to Jacob's."

No, Jacob did not know best. And even more, she was frustrated that he'd asked Mary to come here, walking all this way on her sore hip. Striving for patience wasn't easy, but she did her best. "I will walk you home, Mary. There is no reason to trouble you by having you come to Jacob's. I plan to stay here at my home tonight."

"Is that wise?" Mary asked with a frown. "Jacob will not be happy, *ain't so*?"

She bit back an unkind reply. "*Komm*, we shall go. What time does Leah usually come home?"

"Half past five, sometimes later." Mary stood and accepted her arm. "*Ach*, Rachel, you remind me of your *mammi*. I miss her friendship."

"I miss her, too." Rachel carefully assisted Mary outside, then down the street to the Moore residence. Her house was between Jacob's farm and the Moore house, but she craned her neck to see if Jacob was around. Thankfully, he was not. She was angry with him for overstepping his bounds by talking to Mary about being a chaperone.

"It was difficult for her after your father left," Mary continued. "My Kaleb helped harvest her crops that year, but it was also the last time she'd farmed the land. She had no heart for that work, *ain't so*?"

"Farmed the land?" Rachel frowned and glanced at Mary. "I remember chickens, but I was not aware we lived on a farm."

"*Ach*, yes. Your father enjoyed farming." Then Mary abruptly changed the subject. "Rachel, I will let Leah know you would like to talk to her. Mayhap she can stop by later?"

"Ja, denke," Rachel answered automatically, her mind still back on the information Mary had provided. Most of Rachel's memories of her mother were related to the house she currently lived in. She'd assumed the animals had been kept nearby. But there was no farmland around the house, so what land had her father toiled?

"Mary, where did my parents live when they were farming?"

The older woman hesitated, then said, "The property is on the far northwest side of the community. Your mother did not wish to stay there after your father left, so she sold the property and purchased the smaller house you live in now."

"I had no idea," Rachel murmured. "I wish I could remember the farm."

"Best that you don't—there's no need to concern yourself with the past, Rachel." They walked in silence for several moments before Mary added, "*Ach*, I should not have mentioned the farm to you. I know your mother did not talk about her life back then."

"I always knew the pain of my *daddi*'s leaving wounded her deeply," Rachel said softly. "But I wish I knew more about him."

"He's not one of us any longer." Mary's expression turned somber. "*Ach*, *Daddi* Moore would be angry I mentioned him at all. Your father was banished for leaving his wife and daughter behind, and that was enough of a burden for your mother to carry, *ain't so*? Please, Rachel, we shall not speak of him again."

"I understand." Rachel knew that being banished by the Amish must have been heartbreaking for her mother. Obviously, that was why her mother hadn't mentioned her father, even to Rachel.

And her mother had been forced to live the rest of her life alone. Divorce was not an option among the Amish, not even when a man abandoned his family. Rachel had expressed concern, but her mother had assured her she was fine living alone. That she in fact preferred it.

Rachel had suspected the real truth was that her mother didn't trust another man not to break her heart. The way her father must have.

Yet despite his being banished and shunned, she couldn't help wishing she understood more about the man who'd married her mother, had a daughter, farmed the land, then ruthlessly turned his back, abandoning his family eighteen years ago.

Mayhap her father's influence was stronger than she'd thought. Mayhap, it was the real reason she was reluctant to settle down with a husband to have children of her own.

Sweat dampened his shirt as the temperature rose throughout the day. Jacob had done his best to stay focused on getting things accomplished, especially repairing his plow so that he could begin planting next week.

Yet in the back of his mind, he was looking forward to seeing Rachel. In truth, he'd been sorely disappointed when she had not been at the house when he'd come in for his midday meal.

He'd eaten alone in his kitchen, all too aware of the emptiness around him. The food was good—Rachel had made fresh bread that morning—but he hadn't enjoyed the fare as much as he had when she'd been there, with him.

Why hadn't she arrived yet? It shouldn't have taken this long for her to bring her things over. Had Mary Moore had trouble getting to Rachel's? He'd offered a ride in his buggy, but Mary had insisted she needed to walk. According to her doctor, it was good for her hip to keep mobile.

He told himself Rachel was probably chatting with Mary, not paying attention to the time. Yet it also occurred to him that Rachel may not be happy he'd asked for Mary Moore's help in acting as a chaperone. But upon learning of Leah's not returning from the Amish Shoppe until late, he did not see an alternative.

Rachel's safety was the most important thing. Certain sure, after seeing the vandalism at her café and knowing the kidnapper was still searching for her, she would not hesitate to comply with his wishes.

When he finished his midday meal, he took a quick break to walk over to Rachel's house. He knocked at the door, but there was no answer. His heart thudded against his chest as he quickly walked inside, calling her name.

She wasn't there. Perplexed, he glanced around the room. A basket was sitting on the counter, but that was the only indication she was still planning to come to his house. He considered taking the basket over himself, but feared Rachel would be alarmed to find it missing.

Disgruntled that she hadn't come to his house as

quickly as promised, he turned to leave. Certain sure she was a maddening woman. Why was she so difficult?

He walked quickly back to his farm, debating whether to go to the Moore residence again. No, he would not chase the woman, especially since he knew Mary would honor his request to be a chaperone.

No doubt, Rachel and Mary were together. Mayhap had even shared the midday meal. He told himself to be grateful that Rachel wasn't alone. She'd suffered enough; a day of visiting with Mary was not much to ask.

Jacob went back to work, trying desperately not to glance continuously at his house to search for signs Rachel and Mary had arrived.

They would be there by dinner, and he would be grateful for whatever meal Rachel prepared for them.

He also kept an eye out for any sign of the white car or blue truck. Thankfully, he did not see either of them. Mayhap Liam would return later to let them know the killer had been arrested.

Although if that was the case, Rachel would not need to come and stay at his home at all. He tried not to focus on the depressing thought.

When he finished for the day, at least until he made his nighttime rounds to check on the livestock, he made his way up to the house. The moment he opened the door, he knew Rachel had not come.

A wave of fear washed over him. What if the killer had taken her? Why hadn't he followed up when she wasn't at her house earlier?

Spinning on his heel, he ran from the house and headed straight for Rachel's. He didn't bother to set up the horse and buggy; despite his long day, he ran fast enough that he still made good time.

The house was exactly the way it was earlier. The basket was still on the counter, and there was no sign of Rachel.

The tiny hairs on the back of his neck rose in alarm. He once again set off at a run, going back to his place. This time he would take the horse and buggy to the Moore residence, just to be sure Rachel wasn't there.

Deep down, he prayed she would be. That his own sheer stubbornness hadn't gotten in the way of her safety.

He quickly bridled his horse and connected him to the buggy. After leaping into the seat, he called, "Giddyap!"

The horse obediently trotted down the driveway on command. He fought to control his emotions as he covered the distance between his home and the Moores'.

Rachel would be there. *Rachel must be there!*

He pulled into the driveway. Jumping down, he wrapped the horse's reins over a fence post and rushed up to knock at the door.

"Jacob!" Mary greeted him warmly. "You must be looking for Rachel."

"I am." His overwhelming fear melted away, leaving a spurt of anger in its place. "I expected you both to be at my place by now."

"*Ach*, she told me she was staying at her place instead." Mary spread her hands. "Rachel made me a lovely meal, then returned home."

A wave of fear washed over him. "She's not there, I looked."

Mary frowned. "That's strange. She left here about fifteen minutes ago."

Fifteen minutes? He tried to take heart that she hadn't been missing for hours. Mayhap she wasn't missing at all. "Did she mention stopping to visit anyone else?"

"Not that I recall," Mary said.

He struggled to remain calm as he considered the possibilities. Had he missed her along the way? Had she taken a shortcut back to her house? "I will ride along the road, see if I can find her."

"Certain sure she's fine, Jacob," Mary assured him.

He nodded, then hurried back to his buggy. Rachel would be fine if she would simply listen to him. But *ach*, no, she did not have the common sense to follow reasonable guidelines to stay safe.

Fifteen minutes. Still long enough to have been kidnapped.

He drove the buggy a little slower, raking his gaze over the area for signs of Rachel. She was nowhere in sight, not even at his farm as he passed by.

He went around a curve in the road in time to see a man creeping up toward Rachel's front door.

The kidnapper!

"Hiya!" He slapped the reins, then shouted, "Rachel, look out!"

Jacob quickly pulled his hunting rifle from the buggy floorboard. Holding the reins in one hand, he lifted the rifle with the other and fired a shot in the air. Mostly to scare the guy away.

His ruse worked. The man spun around and sprinted across the property to where the white car waited. It had been partially hidden by trees or he'd have noticed it sooner.

Jacob used both hands on the rifle, aiming at the back end of the vehicle. He fired another shot, but the movement of the buggy made him miss.

The white car raced away, but that was no longer his concern. He pulled up in front of Rachel's house, leaped from the buggy and ran inside, calling her name.

Hoping and praying she wasn't hurt.

EIGHT

Rachel had just returned home after spending time with Mary Moore, when she heard Jacob's shout followed by gunfire.

Reacting instinctively, she ran toward the back bedroom, thinking to crawl through the window to escape. But paused when she heard Jacob call her name a second time, his voice louder.

"Rachel, talk to me. Are you okay?" His voice boomed from the front of the house, and she cautiously moved through to peer into the kitchen.

"Jacob?" Her eyes widened when she saw him standing there, breathing heavily while carrying a rifle. "Did you fire that shot?"

"*Ja*, to scare the man off. He left in the white car. Certain sure you're not hurt?" His anxious gaze raked over her, but then turned into a grim scowl. "Where have you been? Did you realize the kidnapper was outside your door?"

She paled and shook her head. "No, I did not. He was outside? You saw him?"

"Yes, although I'm surprised he made such a bold

move before the sun had gone down." Jacob glanced over to where her basket of goods still sat on the counter. "*Komm*, we must go."

She wanted to protest, to let him know she did not appreciate his asking Mary to be a chaperone, but sensed he was hanging on to his anger by a thread. And, she was forced to admit, with good reason. Certain sure she had not anticipated the man would come to her home.

Even Liam had thought she would be safe here among the Amish.

How had the killer known where she lived?

She remembered the break-in at the café. Her paperwork had been disturbed, not ruined, but moved about. Paperwork which listed her home address. Even within the Amish they had ways to identify where a home was located.

Her shoulders slumped as she realized how foolish she'd been. Her desire to remain independent had put Jacob in the position to rush to her rescue.

Thankfully, God had watched over him, protecting Jacob from being harmed.

"*Denke*, Jacob," she said softly. Walking over to the kitchen, she picked up the basket. "Certain sure I'm ready to go with you now."

He seemed surprised at her easy agreement, stepping forward to take the basket from her hand. *"Sehr gut."* He gave a nod, then turned toward the door.

The horse and buggy were outside, the reins lying on the ground. It made her feel guilty all over again as she imagined Jacob jumping off the buggy to rush inside.

Jacob set his rifle and the basket inside the buggy, then went over to pick up the reins. He took a moment to check the horse, running his hands over the animal's legs to be sure he was not injured.

Finally, he turned to help her inside. She avoided his gaze as she took his hand, not wanting to see the anger and frustration she was sure were reflected in his eyes.

He climbed in beside her, then turned the horse to head back down the road. "You failed to answer my question. Where have you been?"

"Visiting with Mary Moore. You asked her to be a chaperone, *ain't so*?" She kept her tone mild, since this was not the time to express her concern.

"I came here earlier, but you were not home. Then I went to the Moore farm, but you weren't there, either. I—" his voice faltered "—I feared you had been kidnapped."

"*Ach*, Jacob, I'm sorry." She lightly touched his arm. "I admit I was angry that you asked Mary to come see me, telling her of the need for a chaperone so that I might be safe. I thought we had an agreement…" Her voice trailed off. "It doesn't matter now. Please know I very much regret causing you concern."

He nodded, then pulled back on the reins, stopping the buggy near his house. "I need you to tell me what you would like me to do as far as providing for your safety."

Humbling that he'd asked for her input. "We need to go to the Moores' and see if either Leah or Mary can stay with us, *ja*?"

He turned his head. Their gazes met and clung. Attraction sizzled between them, stealing her breath and making her wonder why she cared about this man who frustrated her to no end.

Yet a moment later, the awareness was gone. "As you wish."

The ride back to the Moore property didn't take long and they ran into Leah along the way. Rachel smiled at her friend. "Leah, would you like a ride?"

"Ja, denke." Leah climbed into the buggy beside Rachel, causing her to inch closer to Jacob. The heat radiating from him was distracting. "Where are you headed?"

"Your home. I— *Ach*, we have a favor to ask." Rachel glanced at Jacob, then back to Leah. "Would you be willing to stay at Jacob's tonight as a chaperone?"

"Certain sure, but why?" Leah's curious gaze bounced between them. "Is there a problem at your house, Rachel?"

"*Ach*, no, but it appears I am in danger." She swallowed hard, and added, "Someone has tried to kidnap me. It is not prudent for me to remain at my home alone."

"Kidnap?" Leah's eyes widened in horror. "When?"

"Yesterday." It felt much longer than twenty-four hours since the attack had happened. "I know it's a lot to ask of a friend, and I will understand if you say no."

"Of course I will stay with you and Jacob," Leah said quickly. She patted Rachel's hands. "I will need a few minutes to pack my things, *ja*?"

"*Denke.* We appreciate your helping Rachel in this way." Jacob spoke for the first time since picking up Leah from the side of the road. "Certain sure you will both be safe at my farm."

"I know we will," Leah agreed.

Jacob followed them inside, but stayed back as Rachel and Leah explained the new plan to her *mammi*.

As they packed a satchel for Leah, her friend said, "I'm surprised Jacob has offered to have us stay with him. Usually, he values his privacy."

Rachel managed a smile. "He saved me from harm on several occasions recently. Certain sure he feels obligated now to continue in his role as protector."

"Mayhap he seeks to court you." Leah lifted a brow. "He is a widower and allowed to remarry should he choose."

"*Ach*, no! Certain sure I would be the last person Jacob would wish to court." Rachel felt her cheeks go hot. This was why she hadn't wanted the entire community to know of the danger, and Jacob's offer to have her stay with him. "Know this, Leah, we are not together in that way. He is often vexed by me, and the feeling is mutual."

"Mayhap, but I think you must be important to him, or he wouldn't have gone out of his way to help you." Leah looped her bag over her arm. "You realize I must go to the Amish Shoppe again in the morning."

"*Ja*, I know." In this way, she and Leah were much alike. Leah ran the Sunshine Café, taking her responsibilities seriously. "I will ask Jacob to give you a ride, so you don't have to be up as early."

"*Denke*, a buggy ride would be much appreciated." Leah led the way down to the main living area, taking a moment to give her mother a quick hug. "Good night, *Mammi*. Be careful not to injure your hip, and send word if you need something."

Mary smiled. "I'll be fine, *ain't so*? *Daddi* Ezekiel will be home later, if you'd like to talk to him."

"Denke," Rachel said, throwing Jacob a knowing

glance. No doubt he'd asked about needing to speak with the elder.

As they headed back, she heard Jacob's stomach rumbling with hunger, and felt guilty all over again that she hadn't cooked as promised. "I will make dinner soon."

Jacob nodded, but didn't say anything more. As soon as he pulled into his driveway, she was thinking about what she'd brought and what Jacob had that she could make into a meal.

After Jacob carried their belongings inside and returned to care for his horse, she and Leah went to work. Rachel enjoyed spending time with her friend, who was a good cook, too, but her senses were attuned to Jacob, waiting for his return.

Deep down, she wondered what would happen if Jacob wished to court her. He was frustrating, kind, opinionated, protective and demanded his way more often than not.

Yet she couldn't deny that based on recent events, she would be lost without him.

Jacob's thoughts whirled as he cared for his horse. The killer had learned which home was Rachel's and if Jacob had been even five minutes later, would have succeeded in kidnapping her.

Liam needed to know what happened, but he had no way of contacting the sheriff now. Mayhap tomorrow, Liam would return to the community to update them on his progress in finding the man in the sketch, along with either the white car or blue truck.

He could also let David and Elizabeth McKay know

of the new attempt on Rachel. They would be heading to the Amish Shoppe in the morning and could contact Liam when they arrived.

The elders would need to know, too. Ezekiel hadn't been home, but he would make sure Rachel performed her duty to explain what was going on first thing tomorrow.

This near abduction had taken place here, within their community. As such the elders deserved to know of the potential threat.

A wave of exhaustion hit hard as he trudged back to the house. It wasn't the physical labor he'd performed; that was nothing out of the ordinary.

No, it was the emotional turmoil that had taken its toll. Something he hadn't experienced in a long time.

Since losing Anna and Isaac.

Jacob had always preferred to keep his emotions in a deep freeze. His life had fallen into a comfortable routine, without worrying about anything other than his farm.

Somehow, Rachel Miller had blasted through his defenses. For the first time in a long while, he cared about someone else's well-being. Felt responsible to keep Rachel, and Leah, too, safe from harm.

God had brought him to this moment, he knew. It had not been an easy road after losing his family. He hadn't blamed God, but he had blamed himself. He knew it must be his fault that his wife and son were taken away from him.

And had lived without joy as penance, ever since.

Upon entering his home, the sound of laughter hit

hard. For an instant he could hear Anna's laughter, but she and Isaac were with God now.

No, it was Leah and Rachel laughing. Despite his weariness, he almost smiled.

"Dinner smells *sehr gut*." He crossed to the sink to wash his hands.

Leah and Rachel set several bowls on the table, then took seats on either side of him. It was disconcerting to have two women in his home, and he did his best not to stick his foot in his mouth, inadvertently upsetting them.

The way he usually did.

He bowed his head. "Heavenly Father, we thank You for providing this food for us to eat. Please continue to guide us to safety, amen."

"Amen," Rachel and Leah echoed.

Jacob realized he'd prayed more in the past few days with Rachel than he had in the entire two years Anna and Isaac had been gone. Oh, he'd attended services, listening to Bishop Bachman's sermons and teaching, but he hadn't done much praying on his own.

"Jacob, I hope your horse was not injured from the events earlier," Rachel said.

He picked up his fork and began to eat. The food was delicious, much better than he'd anticipated. "The animal is fine." He darted a glance at Leah. "You've told Leah of the danger?"

"*Ja*, she deserves to know."

"So do the elders, *ain't so*?" He tried not to sound overbearing. "The danger is here now, not just at your café."

"That is true," Rachel reluctantly agreed.

Leah nodded. "*Ja*, we can walk over to visit with my *grosspappi* after we finish our meal. *Mammi* said he'd be home later, *ain't so*?"

Rachel hesitated, clearly not expecting her friend to suggest they go visit her grandfather tonight. Jacob expected her to argue, but she didn't. "Of course, if you think that is best."

"He will discuss the matter with the rest of the elders and Bishop Bachman. It's best to make sure everyone in the community is on alert for *Englisch* strangers, *ain't so*?" Leah said.

"Yes, of course," Rachel agreed.

Jacob was glad to know that Rachel planned to do what was necessary. The Amish were usually aware when *Englischers* came through, but it would be more important now than ever, considering the kidnapper who'd sneaked up to Rachel's home.

Why hadn't Liam or his deputies found him from the sketch?

After they finished eating, they set out. Jacob carried his rifle, making sure to walk several paces behind the women. Rachel and Leah chatted about various recipes as they walked side by side. Once everyone knew the two women were staying with him, Leah serving as a chaperone, some would gossip about a possible courtship.

Too bad, they would be sorely disappointed. As soon as Liam had arrested this man, he and Rachel would no longer have a need to interact.

A surprisingly depressing thought.

Ezekiel Moore shared a home with his daughter-in-law Mary and granddaughter, Leah. It occurred to

Jacob that Rachel could have simply moved in with the Moore family, rather than asking Leah to come to Jacob's.

But no, he did not wish to bring danger to the Moore family. Bad enough that Leah would be staying as he protected Rachel. Ezekiel's wise guidance was needed among the elders, there was no reason to place the elderly man in harm's way.

When they entered the home, he found Ezekiel sitting in the living room near Mary, who was mending some clothing. The older man stood and stepped forward to greet them.

"*Ach*, what brings you here?" Ezekiel asked.

Jacob glanced at Mary, who continued sewing. It seemed as if she had not filled her father-in-law in on what little she knew. Which was probably for the best, as Ezekiel needed to hear the whole story, from the beginning.

"I need to speak with you," Rachel said, stepping forward. "There have been several incidents that you and the other elders need to be aware of."

"I see." Ezekiel gestured to the kitchen table. "Let's sit down."

Rachel looked nervous, but Jacob was impressed by her determination to come forward. He knew it couldn't be easy. After she explained about the murder she'd witnessed, the man in the blue truck pointing a gun at them and the attempted kidnapping, Ezekiel's dark eyes widened with shock and surprise.

"And you have no idea who this man is?" the elder asked.

"I don't." Rachel sighed and rubbed her temple. "I

wish I did. It's most frustrating to have someone coming after you without any clue as to why."

Ezekiel stared at her for a long moment. "Am I to understand you did not recognize this man? He had not been a customer in your café?"

She looked uncertain for a moment, then shook her head. "I don't believe so. I don't know all my customers by face, but I think I would have recognized him, especially if he'd been there recently."

Ezekiel nodded thoughtfully, turning to look out the window. Jacob wondered what the elder was thinking, but felt it was impolite to ask.

"*Ach*, you are wise to stay with Jacob and Leah," Ezekiel finally said. "Your café will remain closed, *ja*?"

Rachel lowered her gaze and nodded. "Until this man has been arrested."

Another long pause, before Ezekiel glanced at him. "Jacob, I appreciate your willingness to provide Rachel and Leah the safety they need."

"Of course." Jacob sensed the meeting had come to a close. "Please let me know if you need anything further, *ja*?"

"I will discuss this safety concern with the rest of the council tomorrow." Ezekiel stood and made his way back to his chair. "Good night."

"Good night, *Grosspappi*." Leah gave her grandfather a smile, then led the way outside.

Darkness had fallen as they made their way back. Jacob wondered again why the kidnapper had shown up so early, unless he was trying to make sure he had the correct house, so as to avoid making a mistake in taking the wrong woman.

He mulled that over as they walked. It took him a moment to realize the route Rachel had taken brought them through several yards so that they were passing the back of her house.

Was this how he'd missed her earlier?

A flash of light caught his eye. He froze, then softly called, "Rachel, Leah, stop."

The two women froze, then slowly turned to face him. "Is something wrong?" Rachel asked in a whisper.

He continued to watch the house, waiting for the flash of light to reappear. He didn't think he'd imagined it, yet it had come and gone so fast, he couldn't be sure his mind hadn't played tricks on him.

There! He saw it again, and this time, Rachel did, too.

"Jacob, someone is inside," she whispered.

"I know." He didn't want to leave them alone, but he also didn't want the kidnapper to get away again. "Hurry, go back to the Moore home. I'll check inside the house."

"Wait." Rachel grabbed his arm in a tight grip. "What if there are two men inside?"

He appreciated her concern, but thankfully still carried his hunting rifle. Never in his life had he aimed a weapon at another man and did not relish the possibility now. "Please go."

"*Komm*, Rachel," Leah whispered.

Rachel released his arm, taking a step back. He quickly moved toward Rachel's house, envisioning the layout in his mind's eye. He had only been inside a handful of times, and never in her private rooms. But he knew where the back door was located.

He sent up a silent prayer for God to watch over Rachel and Leah as he stepped closer to the back door. He listened intently but didn't hear anything.

If there were two men inside, they were being extremely quiet.

He silently opened the back door, wincing when he realized it wasn't locked. He hadn't reminded Rachel to do so, and it was not a common practice in their community, either.

He kept his rifle in the crook of his arm, watching for the flickering light to give him a clue as to where the intruder may be. He froze when he heard a gravelly voice.

"The place is empty. Let's get out of here."

Hearing footsteps, Jacob shouted, "Stop!"

A loud bang indicated the front door had been flung open. Jacob rushed forward, his rifle at the ready, but something hit him hard on the back of his head. Knocked off balance, he dropped the rifle and fell to the floor, struggling to remain conscious.

As darkness shrouded his vision, his last thought was to pray Rachel was safe with the Moore family.

NINE

"Wait, we have to go back." Rachel stopped in the middle of the field, resisting Leah's attempt to pull her forward. The urge to return to her house was strong. What if there were two men and they overpowered Jacob?

"No, Jacob told us to get to safety." Leah's eyes were wide with fear. "We can send my *grosspappi* to check on him."

Rachel shook her head. "Leah, I cannot put your *grosspappi* at risk. Run ahead, and I'll go back on my own."

Leah sighed then shook her head. "No. I cannot let you go alone. We'll be safer together, *ain't so*?"

Rachel wished she could agree with her friend, but she didn't feel safe at all. Not now, and not going back to her house, where someone lurked inside. Yet she could not ignore the voice in the back of her mind, telling her Jacob needed help.

"Mayhap we can cause a distraction," Rachel whispered as they hurried back through the darkness. Stars sprinkled the sky, and the half-moon provided some light. But not much.

Large rocks tripped her several times, forcing her to slow her pace lest she or Leah fall and twist an ankle. As they grew closer to her home, she searched for the flashing light, indicating someone was still inside.

But she saw nothing.

"Where is Jacob?" Leah whispered.

"I don't know." The silence was eerie, and she wondered if the kidnappers had taken Jacob with them for some reason. She opened the back door and peered inside.

Seeing nothing alarming, she ventured farther. An instant later, she saw the dark form sprawled on the ground. She froze, wondering if it was one of the kidnappers, when the man let out a low groan.

Not the kidnapper. "Jacob!" She rushed to his side, dropping to her knees beside him. "Jacob, are you injured? Can you hear me?"

Jacob groaned, then lifted his head, glancing around in confusion. She took his arm and tried to help him up.

"Rachel? What are you doing here?" His voice was low and husky as he staggered to his feet. Leah picked up the hunting rifle from the floor. He leaned against the wall, as if to get his bearings.

"*Ach*, it's a good thing we came back, *ain't so*? Leah, will you take his other arm? We need to walk back to his farm."

"I'm fine," he protested, but she ignored him. Her heart had squeezed painfully in her chest when she'd realized he'd been lying on the floor, hurt. And knew this was why she'd felt the need to return.

"*Komm*, Jacob. Take it slow, *ja*?" Rachel took Jacob's arm and draped it across her shoulders.

"I'm fine." His words were stronger now, although he still leaned on her for support. "*Ach*, you and Leah were supposed to be with the Moore family."

"Rachel is stubborn, *ain't so*?" Leah said in a light tone. She carried the rifle while supporting Jacob's other side. "She insisted we return to look for you."

"And it was the right thing to do," Rachel said firmly. Who knows how long Jacob would have been on the floor? There was no sign of the kidnappers, other than her open front door, but she knew they must have injured Jacob.

What if they had killed him? She shivered at the thought.

They left the house and walked toward Jacob's farm. No one spoke for several minutes. Once they'd gotten over the rutted fields, she asked, "Do you remember what happened?"

"There were two men in the house," Jacob said quietly. "I heard them say you weren't there."

Another shiver skated down her spine. It was no surprise they had been searching for her, but the realization of what might have happened if she'd stayed home alone was frightening.

"I heard the two men talking. I shouted at them to stop, hoping I could get a better look, when I was struck from behind. I misjudged where the two men were. I assumed both were in the living room and had left together, but one had been in the bedroom. Before I realized it, he struck me on the back of the head." Disgust lined Jacob's tone. "That is the last thing I remember."

"I'm glad you were not hurt worse." She pushed the

words through a tight throat. She was upset to know he'd been injured because of her.

Once they reached Jacob's house, he made his way to the sofa. He closed his eyes and murmured, "I'll stay here for a while."

Leah set the rifle against the wall, then carried her bag to the guest room. Rachel ran a cloth under cold water, then brought it for Jacob. "Try this, see if it helps."

He opened his eyes and stared at her for a long moment. Their faces were so close, she found herself drawn to him in a way she'd not experienced before. All too soon, Jacob averted his gaze. He took the cold cloth from her fingers and pressed it against the back of his head. *"Denke."*

"Wilkom." Her voice sounded breathless, and she tried to shake off the strange awareness. Of course she cared about his welfare, the same way she would for anyone within their Amish community.

Yet she could not deny this intensity of emotion was different. It was—personal.

There was no reason to be drawn to Jacob in this way. She liked him as a friend, but they were too different for anything more.

He'd closed his eyes again, his face pulled in a grimace that indicated he was in pain. She felt terrible about his injury, but all she could do now was take care of him. Realizing she'd been staring at him for several minutes, she inwardly sighed and forced herself to turn away.

Enough foolishness. She went to check on Leah, who had made herself at home in the guest room. "Is there anything you need?" Rachel asked.

"No, I'm fine." Leah's eyes flashed in concern. "Jacob will be all right?"

"*Ja*, he has a hard head, *ain't so*?" Rachel tried for a light tone, even though she shared Leah's concern. "I will keep an eye on him overnight to make sure he does not take a turn for the worse."

Leah nodded. "Remember, I will be up early to get to the Amish Shoppe."

Rachel winced. "I'm not sure if Jacob will be able to give you a ride as I had hoped."

"There is no need to be concerned, I have walked many times," Leah assured her. "I am always up early, *ain't so*?"

As Rachel usually walked to her café, too, she understood. "Good night, Leah. Sleep well."

"You, too, Rachel."

Rachel returned to the kitchen. She straightened and cleaned, more to keep herself busy than out of necessity. Jacob remained so quiet, she worried he'd slipped unconscious again. Tiptoeing to the sofa, she watched the rise and fall of his chest, grateful his breathing was even.

She didn't want to wake him, but felt certain it would not be good to have him unconscious. When she rested her hand on his shoulder, he opened his eyes.

"*Ach*, sorry to disturb you," she apologized.

"No need." He looked around in surprise. "I must have fallen asleep."

"*Komm*, you need to go to your room and lie down." Rachel gestured to the sofa. "You are too tall to sleep here."

After handing her the damp cloth that was no longer cool to the touch, he rose, swaying a bit as he did so. She slipped her arm around his waist to steady him.

To her surprise, he didn't reject her support. He glanced down at her at the same moment she looked up at him. He bent his head and lightly kissed her temple. "I'm glad you're here, Rachel."

"I, uh, am glad to be here, too." Flustered by the completely unexpected and sweet kiss, she could feel her cheeks growing warm with embarrassment. Certain sure he meant the kiss as a gesture of thanks, not from any romantic interest.

They moved down the hall to the bedrooms. It was strange to be in Jacob's personal space, but she told herself to remain focused on his injury.

"Denke," he murmured as he sat on the edge of the bed. "I will be fine from here."

"Of course." She took a step back, then hesitated. "I feel the need to check on you throughout the night."

He frowned, then lifted his hand to touch the back of his head. "*Ja*, that will be fine."

"Sehr gut." She turned and closed the door behind her. Then stood for a moment, lifting her fingertips to the spot on her temple that he'd kissed.

Somehow, Jacob's injury had shifted the foundation of their relationship. In truth, she was more comfortable arguing with him than caring for him.

Even though she knew this new arrangement of staying together in Jacob's home was necessary, she felt certain things would not go back to normal once the danger was over.

No, from this point forward, she sensed she'd feel

a certain kinship with Jacob. A connection that would last long after the danger had passed.

And certain sure she had no idea what to do about it.

The pounding in Jacob's head made it difficult to think clearly. It was the only excuse he could come up with for kissing Rachel on the temple.

He took off his boots and stretched out on the bed fully dressed to preserve Rachel's modesty when she came to check on him. He wouldn't have agreed to her doing such a task if not for the fear he had of falling asleep and never waking up.

After pulling one of Elizabeth McKay's quilts over himself, he closed his eyes. He hoped the pain would be better by the time he needed to do his morning chores. He did not think Leah and Rachel could handle the work without him, and he did not want to cause more work for others in the community.

Several times during the night, he felt Rachel's light touch on his shoulder. He always assured her he was fine, and as time passed, the pain in his head lessened.

It wasn't gone by morning, but it was tolerable. He quickly changed out of his wrinkled clothes into fresh things, pulled on his boots, then followed the scent of coffee to find Rachel working in the kitchen.

To his surprise, the sun was already lightening the sky. "*Ach*, I overslept."

"Certain sure you look much better for the extra hour of sleep," Rachel said firmly. She poured him a cup of coffee and he sipped it gratefully. "I will help you with the morning chores, but will need direction as I have little experience in caring for livestock."

"No need, I can do the work myself." He took another sip of his coffee, then reached for his hat. It was badly misshapen after the assault by the kidnappers. He frowned, then glanced down the hall toward the guest room. "Where is Leah?"

"She walked to the Amish Shoppe with David and Elizabeth." Rachel dried her hands on a towel and turned to face him. "I insist on helping, Jacob. I'm waiting for the bread to rise anyway, so the early-morning meal will be delayed. Besides, we will get the chores finished much faster by working together, *ain't so*?"

He couldn't argue with her logic. He thought she could gather eggs from the chickens, while he took care of the horses and cattle.

Despite the lingering headache, he found himself enjoying the morning chores, especially working alongside Rachel. She managed to avoid being pecked by the chickens as she gathered eggs. After she carried them into the house, she returned to muck stalls.

He was secretly amazed at how she attacked each chore with a smile and steely determination to do her best. While she was clearly more at home in the kitchen, Rachel did not let the unfamiliar work keep her from participating.

"I can do the rest," Jacob said, when she'd finished with the stalls. "I would very much appreciate a meal. Certain sure my stomach is growling with hunger."

She laughed, and for the first time in what seemed like forever, he felt a responding smile tugging at his lips. "I will be glad to go inside to cook for you, Jacob."

"Sehr gut," he managed, his pulse racing as if he'd

been running, rather than leaning on a pitchfork and chatting with Rachel.

He watched her walk to the house, then turned his attention to his chores. It had been a long time since anyone had helped him muck stalls, and he was surprised at how nice it was to have company while doing such a mundane task.

Even Anna had not done much with the livestock once Isaac was born. He wished he knew why she'd been leaving him the day she and Isaac had been killed in the buggy accident. At the time, he'd been preoccupied about the drought impacting the corn, so he knew it was his fault she hadn't approached him.

Still, he wished Anna had voiced her concerns. He'd thought their relationship was good. But obviously, he'd been wrong.

About that, and mayhap about other things, too.

Jacob told himself to let go of the past. He would never know why Anna and Isaac were so far away when they'd been struck by the car. And even if he did know, it would not change the outcome.

Bishop Bachman had counseled him to let go of his anger and grief, while trusting in God's plan. Something he had not found easy to do. For a full year he'd thought of little else aside of what he'd lost.

Over the second year, his grief had faded to a dull throb, yet he would still occasionally experience a flash of anger. Most aimed at himself. Certain sure he must have done something for which he was being punished.

Now he began to realize that God's plan must have been for him to protect Rachel from harm. There was no denying this role gave him a keen sense of purpose, something more important than simply surviving from day to day.

Being clobbered on the head was just part of the job. He was grateful he was the one who'd been hurt rather than Rachel.

He quickly finished the morning chores and headed inside. The enticing scent of fresh bread welcomed him, and he once again found himself smiling.

"*Ach*, you're just in time, Jacob." Rachel glanced at him over her shoulder. "The meal is ready."

"*Denke*, Rachel, everything smells delicious." He washed his hands and face, then took a seat at the table. "Too bad Leah isn't here to enjoy this, too."

"Leah wanted to open her café on time," Rachel said as she brought the eggs, toast and jam to the table. "But mayhap tomorrow we can break our fast together."

"Please let Leah know that I can take her to the Amish Shoppe tomorrow, *ja*?"

She nodded and took a seat beside him. She rested her hand on his, the warmth of her fingers distracting him from the blessing.

He cleared his throat and tried to gather his thoughts. "Heavenly Father, we thank You for protecting us last evening from those who would cause us harm. We ask for Your continued strength and guidance as we seek truth and justice. Please bless this food we are about to eat, amen."

"Amen," Rachel echoed. "*Sehr gut*, Jacob."

He didn't like admitting the prayers came easier with Rachel beside him. Mayhap God's plan was also to bring Jacob closer to his faith. Something he should not have turned his back on in the first place.

They had just finished their meal when he heard a car engine outside. Immediately, he jumped to his feet, fearing the white car had returned.

But it was Liam's SUV that pulled into his driveway. He frowned, hoping the Green Lake County sheriff was bringing good news to share.

Not bad.

Rachel joined him outside, as if they were a team facing whatever news awaited them together. He was tempted to hold her hand but felt self-conscious after that kiss he'd given her last night.

Mayhap his head injury was worse than he realized. This need to comfort Rachel was very strange.

Liam's expression was solemn when he slid out from behind the wheel. Jacob stepped outside to greet him. "Liam, what brings you here this morning?"

Liam looked surprised by the question, his gaze moving to Rachel.

"I asked David and Elizabeth to contact Liam," Rachel said. "I felt he should know about how the kidnappers were searching for me, and how they assaulted you, Jacob."

Clearly Rachel had been busy while he'd been sleeping in. And since he'd planned on contacting Liam anyway, he simply nodded. "*Komm*, Liam. Are you hungry? Rachel has made plenty of food."

"I would never say no to Rachel's cooking," Liam said with a smile.

"Please, sit down." Jacob took his usual chair, while Rachel prepared a plate for Liam. "I am very concerned that the kidnappers know where Rachel lives. They were searching her house last night. I tried to stop them, but one struck me in the back of the head."

"I heard about your injury from David," Liam admitted. "I'm sorry you were hurt, but you know it could have been much worse, Jacob. They may have killed you."

Rachel's expression turned grim. "*Ach*, I feared that, too, Liam. Please tell me you have learned more about these men who are trying to kidnap me."

"I wish I could." Liam took a moment to eat a slice of fresh bread smothered in jam. "Rachel, what do you know about your father, Peter Miller?"

Rachel stared at him, then said, "Nothing. Mary Moore mentioned that he was a farmer, information I didn't remember. I was only four years old when he abandoned us. I asked her to tell me more, but she changed the subject. As he was shunned and banished from the community, no one will speak about him. Why do you ask?"

Liam ate for a moment, then said, "My parents left the Amish community when I was five years old, and I only have vague memories of your parents. Maybe I'm grasping at straws, but these kidnapping attempts seem to be personal. As if there's more going on than you being a simple witness to a murder."

Jacob frowned, nodding in agreement. "Now that you mention it, I vaguely remember Rachel's father, too. I am three years older than Rachel, but still the images are not clear in my mind."

"You think my father is involved in these kidnapping attempts?" Rachel's voice rose incredulously. "Why would he do such a thing?"

"I'm not sure they are related—it's just one angle to investigate." Liam finished his breakfast, then pushed his plate away. "I keep finding connections to Chicago, and it made me wonder if your father was originally from that area."

"I have no idea," Rachel said wearily. "No one has spoken of him since he left eighteen years ago."

"You don't know your father or where he was originally from, but certain sure the elders would." As soon as Jacob made the comment, he understood it wasn't that simple.

It was highly unlikely the elders would discuss a former member of the Amish community who had been shunned and banished.

TEN

"Do you think so?" Rachel glanced at Jacob. As usual, he was not smiling; his expression was guarded and difficult to read. "Mayhap we can ask Ezekiel Moore what he knows about my father?"

"I know the elders usually don't talk about those who have been banished and shunned," Liam said. "But maybe Ezekiel or the others will bend the rules if the information will help prevent more danger from coming to the community."

"That is a possibility," Jacob agreed.

She reached over to rest her hand on his arm. "*Denke*, Jacob. I would very much appreciate your help in this. You were attacked in my home and sustained a head injury. Certain sure Ezekiel will listen to you."

"I will do my best, but I cannot say for certain sure the elders will see it this way." Jacob covered her hand with his, and the warmth of his touch radiated up her arm. Strange to be so aware of him, when up until recently she hadn't liked him much.

"Mayhap not, but we must try, *ain't so*?" She tried not to let her emotional reaction to him spiral out of control.

Jacob was not interested in a personal relationship; he was just being kind and supportive.

The way he would be with anyone in a similar situation.

The realization had her slipping her hand from beneath his in an effort to pull herself together. "Is there something I can help you with before we visit the Moore family? I don't mind learning new things."

Jacob hesitated for a moment, then shook his head. "*Denke*, but no. I have to do a few more tasks yet, then we will head over to call on Ezekiel."

Despite the way she was desperate to find out all she could about the father she barely remembered, she nodded. "*Sehr gut.* I will clean up the kitchen while you work."

"Please let me know if you discover anything helpful." Liam rose to his feet. "I will keep looking for information on our end, but I am concerned about your safety."

"I will not be caught unaware again," Jacob said grimly.

"I know." Liam gestured to the hunting rifle propped against the wall. "Keep your weapon handy."

Rachel shivered at the thought of Jacob needing to use the rifle against the men who'd tried to kidnap her. She considered moving into the apartment above her café to keep him safe. Although it almost seemed too late. The men would continue to search for her here, within the Amish community. Her leaving would not change that.

Jacob walked Liam outside, leaving her to her cleaning and her troublesome thoughts. It didn't seem reasonable that her father could have anything to do with these events, yet she could see why Liam wanted to rule out the possibility.

She hadn't thought of her father for years, except in passing. Mostly out of her curiosity about the *Englischers* and what had drawn him back to that world.

Now she couldn't wait to learn more about him.

After she'd cleaned the kitchen spotless, she made more bread for Jacob and found some dried meat to use in a beef-and-vegetable soup. Cooking always calmed her nerves, and she relaxed as time slipped by.

Ninety minutes later, Jacob returned to the house. After washing up at the sink, he turned to her with a rare smile. "*Ach*, something smells *sehr gut*."

"The midday meal is ready when we are." She dried her hands on a towel. "Ready to go?"

"Ja." Jacob's smile faded. "We'll take the buggy. I have it waiting outside."

"It's not far," she protested.

"No, but it's safer for us, *ain't so*?" Jacob settled his hat on his head. "Let's go."

The trip didn't take long. When they arrived she saw Mary through the window, sewing. Silently praying Ezekiel would be home, she let Jacob help her down from the buggy.

"Ach, wilkom," Mary greeted them. "Another visit so soon?"

"We would like to speak with Ezekiel if he's available," Jacob said.

"*Komm*, he's here." Mary stepped back and gestured for them to come inside.

"*Ach*, what brings you here?" Ezekiel asked.

Rachel let Jacob take the lead. He stepped forward and joined the elder on the sofa. "We spoke of the danger to Rachel. Last night, I saw a light flickering in the house. When I went to investigate, I was assaulted and knocked unconscious."

Ezekiel's dark eyes grew somber. "*Ach*, the kidnappers know where Rachel lives."

"They do." Jacob lightly touched the back of his head. "But they don't know me, and I will protect Leah and Rachel from harm. However, in speaking with Liam, he believes there is a connection to Peter Miller."

"Peter Miller is dead," Ezekiel said bluntly.

Stunned, Rachel gasped. "He is?"

Ezekiel turned to look at her, then glanced at Mary. After a long moment, he clarified. "Peter Miller is dead to us, as he no longer exists in our community. He died the day he left."

She wondered why Liam wasn't shunned, but thought it may be because he was only a child when his parents had taken him away, and the way he'd fostered his relationship with the Amish as an adult.

"I understand your perspective," Jacob said. "However, Sheriff Harland would like to know if Peter Miller has ties in Chicago. It would be helpful for our community to know if the danger we are seeing now is linked to Rachel's father."

"Rachel's father left eighteen years ago. There is nothing more to tell you." Ezekiel's tone was firm.

Rachel tried not to show her frustration. While Ezekiel claimed there was nothing more to tell, she felt certain there was more to the story around her father's decision to pick up and leave, without looking back.

Unless he had looked back?

Her pulse kicked up as she straightened in her seat. Her mother had a small wooden chest where she'd kept her Bible and other small mementos. She hadn't gone through the items in depth after her mother's passing, but maybe she needed to.

Jacob inclined his head. "*Denke* for your time."

She rose to join Jacob at the door. Ezekiel watched them closely without saying anything as they left, giving her the sense there was something he was holding back.

"I was afraid of that response," Jacob said in a low voice.

"*Ja*, but, Jacob, I remembered something." She grasped his arm with excitement. "My mother's Bible is in a wooden box along with a few other items. I should have thought of it earlier, but mayhap there is something helpful inside."

Jacob hesitated. "Going back to your home is probably not smart."

"We won't stay long." She shook his arm impatiently. "Don't you see? My mother may have something in there related to my father. Certain sure it can't hurt to look. We can bring the entire box to your house if you prefer."

He slowly nodded. "*Sehr gut.* We'll take the buggy and bring the box back with us."

"Denke." She released him, feeling self-conscious. This trip may be futile, but it was an avenue she should have investigated earlier. Especially after Mary Moore had mentioned her father in passing.

For a moment she glanced back at the Moore home,

wondering if Mary would be more willing to tell them what they needed to know.

Mayhap not now that her father-in-law had refused to provide anything helpful. She knew most of the Amish listened to and followed the elders' wishes.

Jacob helped her into the buggy, then headed for her home. The hunting rifle was on the floor at their feet for easy access. It pained her to know he felt the need to carry it with him wherever they went.

Because of her.

The stop didn't take long. Rachel insisted on getting the box herself while Jacob stood outside with his rifle. The box wasn't too heavy. Back at Jacob's, she carried it inside, then set it on the table in front of the sofa.

Jacob sat beside her as she opened the lid. The first items were embroidered towels her mother had set aside for her wedding. She felt her cheeks grow warm, as she quickly set them aside. Jacob probably wouldn't understand the significance—at least she hoped not.

The next item was her mother's Bible. She carefully lifted it into her lap. Opening the book, she looked for information about her father, but there was nothing written inside.

She was about to set it aside when she noticed a barely perceptible gap in the pages. Opening the Bible to that spot, she found a single sheet of paper that had been tucked inside.

To her surprise, the writing was in *Englisch*, not the Amish native language of Pennsylvania Dutch.

"Who is that from?" Jacob asked, leaning close to peer over her shoulder.

She didn't answer, her gaze already scanning the

short note. It only took a moment for her to realize it had been written by her father.

Dear Arleta,
I am so sorry I brought danger to our doorstep and your peaceful Amish community. I know it's my fault, and as such I had no choice but to leave immediately, to keep you and Rachel safe. If I could go back and change my past, I would, but all I can do is ask for your forgiveness. Please know we are safe and we will think of you and Rachel often.
Sincerely,
Peter

"It's from my father." Her voice was shaky. "He left because of some sort of danger."

"We must show this to Liam," Jacob said.

"Ja." She read the note again, and again. It seemed reasonable to believe the current threat was related to the danger her father mentioned, but what did he mean when he said "we are safe"?

We who? A chill snaked down her spine as she realized that finding this short note presented more questions than answers.

Jacob repeated the words Rachel had spoken over and over in his mind to remember them.

It was clear that Peter Miller had left because of danger, not from a decision of not wanting to be Amish.

The information made him wonder about the day he'd lost Anna and Isaac. He'd always assumed his wife had taken his son, leaving him and the Amish behind to start over. Only they'd been hit by an irresponsible driver and killed instead.

Was he wrong about her motives for leaving? There was no way to know, so he ruthlessly shoved that thought aside to focus on the danger threatening Rachel.

"When David and Elizabeth return, we can ask to borrow their phone to call Liam." He tapped the paper. "Mayhap Peter was from Chicago before he joined the Amish."

"Reading this makes me wonder if my father had joined the community as a way to escape danger." Rachel turned to look up at him. "Much the way Shauna hid with Elizabeth last fall when Shauna was being hunted by a killer. It wouldn't be the first time someone had come to live among the Amish to escape the past."

"*Ja*, that seems a likely scenario."

"Jacob, do you remember if I had any siblings?" Her voice was strained. "I cannot understand why my father reassured my mother he and someone else were safe. Who is the other person he was referring to?"

Jacob shook his head. "I'm sorry, but I don't. I'm only three years older than you are and I don't remember much from those early years. I hate to say this, but I don't even remember your father."

"Well, neither do I, so I guess I can't expect too much from you." She sighed and pushed the box aside. "I wish Ezekiel Moore would have bent the rules enough to tell me what I needed to know. I'm sure he knew my father, and whoever else he'd disappeared with." She frowned. "Mayhap it was his brother, or some other member of his family that left with him."

"That would make sense." Jacob's heart ached for

Rachel. Reading this note had not helped in the way she'd hoped. "The sooner we give this information to Liam, the better."

"I'm surprised to hear you say that," Rachel murmured. "You were so against getting the *Englisch* law enforcement involved."

There was no denying the truth to her words. "Mayhap I was wrong to avoid Liam and his deputies." He took her hand. "I will do whatever is necessary to keep you safe, Rachel."

"I believe you." Her eyes glistened with tears before she blinked them away. "*Komm*, you must be hungry. We shall eat the midday meal, *ja*?"

"Sehr gut." He reluctantly released her hand, wondering why he was so drawn to her. Even the sad memories of Anna and Isaac didn't seem to bother him as much these days. There was no point in living in the past when there was a very real threat looming in the present.

He said grace, the prayer flowing easily from his lips. For the first time in months, he could feel God's presence, a sense of calm washing over him.

Danger may have followed Rachel to their community, but he felt more alive now than ever. And he silently thanked God for bringing Rachel into his life.

"You are lost in your thoughts, Jacob." Rachel's sweet voice drew his attention. It was more than the wonderful meals she cooked for him that pulled at him. Yet the strange awareness was disconcerting.

"You learned there was a reason your father left eighteen years ago." He took another bite of bread. "It makes me wonder if there was a good reason behind what

Anna and Isaac were doing so far from home when they were killed."

Rachel nodded slowly. "*Ach*, Jacob, I'm sure there was a valid reason for them to have been there." She paused for a moment, then said, "Did you not speak with Margaret Kellerman about it? Margaret and Anna were close, *ain't so*?"

"No, I did not speak to anyone." He stared down at his bowl of soup. "I did not want to hear the truth, that Anna was taking Isaac because she no longer wanted to live with me."

"*Ach*, Jacob, no." She took his hand. "I understand why you may have thought that way, but you should have tried to uncover the truth."

"Why? To hear I was a terrible husband and father?" He couldn't hide the bitterness in his tone and felt ashamed. "I'm sorry, that sounded petulant."

"It sounded as if you are blaming yourself for actions of another," Rachel said. "It was not you who caused the buggy accident."

"But it seems as if it was my fault Anna was there at all," he countered. "Normally she did not go places without telling me. But that day, she did." He cleared his throat, adding, "And she took Isaac with her."

Rachel squeezed his hand. "I think you will feel better if you speak with Margaret."

"Mayhap you are right." He looked at their joined hands for a moment, then lifted his gaze to hers. "She tried to speak with me after Anna's and Isaac's passing, but I was not in a place to listen."

In truth, he was ashamed to admit he'd been downright rude to Anna's close friend. Margaret had been grieving the loss of Anna and Isaac, too. But he hadn't been interested in what she had to say.

Or rather, he'd been afraid to hear what she had to say.

"Jacob, you must reach out to mend that relationship. And to learn the truth. It's better to know, than to make up excuses in your head, *ain't so*?"

"*Ja*, you're right. I will talk to Margaret," he promised.

"Sehr gut." When Rachel let him go to eat more of her soup, he keenly felt the loss of her touch.

When the meal was finished, he went to check on the livestock, as was his normal habit. The cows provided food for him and for many in the community. Not to mention milk, to make other products.

The planting he needed to do was mostly to keep the cows fed and he also would put in a vegetable garden. Soon, he'd be working long hours, and it worried him to think the kidnapper may not be caught before then.

He was surprised when Rachel came to join him. "Is there a problem?"

"I was hoping you would teach me about what needs to be done to care for the animals." She gestured to the horses in the pasture. "Since I don't have my café to keep me busy all day, I would like to help."

He was touched by her offer. "You did well with the chickens," he teased.

She rubbed her hands. "I was fast enough not to get pecked, a memory from my childhood. But other than raking stalls, I haven't worked much with the horses. Or the cattle."

"*Komm*, we will meet the horses." He took her hand and led her toward them.

She tripped in a hole, losing her balance. He managed to catch her, pulling her close. When Rachel looked up at him, he found himself staring at her mouth.

Certain sure all rational thought faded from his mind. Somehow, he found himself kissing her sweet lips. And to his shock, she let him.

One of the horses had crossed the pasture, bumping his nose into them, breaking the moment. Jacob raised his head, thinking he owed her an apology for his actions, considering he hadn't even asked to court her, when Rachel smiled.

Her simple smile made his heart pound and sweat bead on his temple. And in that moment, he realized he was in trouble.

Big, big trouble.

ELEVEN

"I—I, uh..." Jacob's stammering was sweet.

"Looks as if the horse wants attention, *ja*?" Rachel couldn't help but smile after their amazing kiss. She found herself looking at Jacob in a whole new light. As a nice man who would make a good husband and father.

As soon as that thought entered her mind, she remembered how he'd demanded she shut down her café. Certain sure he'd been concerned about her safety, but she also knew Jacob did not approve of her business.

No, they were not meant to be together. Her smile faded and she stepped back, looking anywhere but at him. Going down this path would result in heartbreak. Jacob was not the man for her.

No matter how much she enjoyed his kiss.

"The horses are important to running my farm," Jacob said, changing the subject. "I use them not only for the buggy, but also for pulling the plow."

The horses were large and somewhat intimidating, but she wasn't afraid. A faint memory of seeing horses up close flashed in her mind, but when she tried to hang on to the image, it melted away.

Her father's horses? Mayhap. Strange to suddenly remember the horse and not her father. She stroked the animal's silky nose. "They are beautiful."

He frowned. "They are strong, which is what I need for pulling the buggy and the plow, *ain't so*?"

Couldn't they be strong and beautiful? She eyed him curiously. It seemed Jacob viewed the horses and work animals without appreciating their beauty. It made her realize he was still grieving the passing of his wife and son.

All the more reason to keep her distance. She already cared about him too much.

After spending a few moments with the horses, Jacob led the way to the barn. There, she helped clean stalls the way she had the day before.

The afternoon passed by quickly as she learned about milking the eight cows, a task done both morning and evening, as well as caring for the horses. She let Jacob finish the chores as she returned to make the evening meal.

She hummed a hymn as she worked, enjoying the ability to cook even if it was just for three people, including Leah, rather than her café customers.

Thinking about her business brought a kernel of worry. She knew she needed to place her future in God's hands, but she couldn't help wondering when she'd be able to open her café, and if her loyal customers would return.

What if the *Englischers* had found somewhere else to dine?

No, she knew there were always new tourists coming to Green Lake. Many would find her. Reassured, she pushed the worry from her mind and focused on the present. It had only been two days and thankfully in May, not June, July or August, their busiest months.

She would continue to pray that Liam would find the kidnappers very soon, so her life and Jacob's could return to a normal routine. One in which their paths would not cross on a regular basis.

Ach, but she would miss him.

Leah walked up the driveway at the same time Jacob headed to the house from the barn. Each would want a few minutes to wash up, but she had the meal ready to go.

"Good evening, Rachel." Leah appeared more tired than usual.

"*Ach*, are you feeling unwell? You seem worn-out."

"I'm fine, but I may head to bed early." Leah reached up to rub her temple. "I've been dealing with a slight headache today."

"Would you prefer soup? We had some for our noon meal," Rachel offered.

"No need, I'm fine." Leah's smile didn't quite reach her eyes. "How are things here? No more trouble, I hope?"

"So far, so good," she assured her. Jacob stomped his boots on the front porch before coming inside. "Jacob, mayhap you might give Leah a ride to the Amish Shoppe tomorrow morning? She could use a break from walking both ways, *ain't so*?"

He frowned, then hesitated. After a pause, he nodded. "*Ja*, I will give Leah a ride."

"*Denke*, Jacob. Tomorrow is Saturday, and the Amish Shoppe is closed on Sunday." Leah glanced at Rachel.

"Mayhap the kidnapper will no longer be a threat by next week."

"I pray that is so," Rachel agreed. She didn't even want to think about this arrangement dragging on for another full week. "*Komm*, the meal is ready."

Jacob washed up at the sink, then led the prayer. Leah didn't eat very much, and excused herself shortly after they'd finished eating.

"Leah appears ill," Jacob said. "Mayhap she should stay home tomorrow."

She stifled a sigh. "Jacob, Leah's Sunshine Café is very important to our community."

"She should not work if she is not feeling well," he protested.

"And if she's ill, she will make the right decision, *ain't so*?" She tried to smile, although his overbearing nature of thinking he knew best grated on her nerves. "I know she has asked others to help her out if needed." She paused, as an idea came to her. "I can work the café for her."

"You?" Jacob looked shocked. "But—what of the kidnappers?"

"They would not expect to find me at the Amish Shoppe, cooking meals in the Sunshine Café." The more she considered the idea, the more she liked it. She would be doing something good for a friend, while also contributing to the community. "I will discuss the possibility with Leah tomorrow morning, *ja*?"

Jacob's scowl deepened, but he didn't argue, despite the way she was certain sure he wanted to.

She turned her attention to cleaning the kitchen. Jacob offered to help, but she shooed him away. "I can do this. I know you must milk the cows again this evening."

"You are right about that." He hesitated, then added, "I would ask that you stay inside, Rachel."

She nodded in agreement. "Of course."

"Denke." He headed back outside to the barn. She watched through the window over the kitchen sink, wondering why he seemed so set against women working at the Amish Shoppe or her café.

Their community had thrived over the years since the creation of the Amish Shoppe barn as a place to attract tourists. Why not support their efforts for the benefit of all?

It was a mystery for sure.

When the kitchen was spotless, she peeked in on Leah. Her friend was asleep, so she didn't wake her. Instead, she left a note offering to take Leah's place at the Sunshine Café in the morning. If Leah didn't feel better by morning, she hoped her friend would accept her help.

Dusk was falling outside, and she stood at the window, wondering what was keeping Jacob. Was he staying out there longer to avoid speaking with her?

A muffled thud startled her. She froze, trying to see if Jacob had dropped something or had fallen.

There was no sign of him.

A chill snaked down her spine, and she internally debated what to do. She'd promised to stay inside the house, but what if Jacob was hurt? No, she couldn't just stand here, doing nothing.

Still, she waited another minute or two before moving through to the living room. Peering through the window, she searched for signs of a white car or blue truck, but didn't see any vehicles.

Drawing a deep breath, she reached for the door handle. Then paused as she realized the rifle was propped against the wall.

Jacob hadn't taken it with him.

She lifted the gun with two hands. It was heavier than she'd expected. With only a rudimentary knowledge of how the weapon worked, she carried it in her arms the way she'd seen Jacob do, hoping that seeing it would frighten the kidnapper away.

If he was out there.

The thud hadn't been her imagination. Moving cautiously, she opened the door and stepped outside. Seeing nothing alarming, she hurried toward the barn.

There! A dark figure moved along the side of the wall. Jacob? No, the person wasn't wearing a hat.

"Go away!" she shouted, bringing the rifle up and aiming it toward the shadow. "Don't make me shoot!"

The figure froze, then suddenly whirled and came directly toward her.

No! She couldn't bring herself to shoot the gun at him, so she pointed the tip of the weapon up over his head and pulled the trigger. The loud crack of the rifle was enough to have the man spinning away.

The rumble of a car engine in the distance confirmed her fears. The kidnapper had escaped, again.

Yet she also knew that he'd figured out where Jacob lived. And that was not good.

It meant he'd be back, and likely very soon.

Jacob had thrown himself into his evening chores, inwardly fuming over Rachel's announcement that she planned to help Leah in the Amish Shoppe the following day.

He'd been so preoccupied he'd almost gotten kicked by one of the horses. Thankfully the animal had only hit the side of his stall.

Then he'd heard Rachel's shouting followed by the crack of the rifle. Dropping the pitchfork, he ran out of the barn, scanning the area for signs of danger. "Rachel! Where are you? Rachel!"

His heart thundered in his chest as he feared the worst. That the kidnapper had found her.

But then he saw her standing with the rifle pointed at the ground. He mentally thanked God for sparing her as he rushed to her side.

"What happened? Are you hurt?"

"I—I'm fine. I scared him away." Her voice was weak and trembling.

He gently removed the rifle from her grasp. He ejected the shell, then made sure there were additional rounds in the chamber before turning back to face her. "The kidnapper was here? At my house?"

"I—think so, yes." She shivered in the cool evening night. "I didn't see his face, but saw him creeping along the side of the barn. I thought he'd hurt you, Jacob. The loud thudding sound was concerning, so I came out to investigate. When I saw the shadow, I shouted and fired the shot over his head to make him leave."

"*Ach*, Rachel." He used the arm not holding the gun to pull her close. "I'm sorry you had to do that. But it worked, *ain't so*? He's gone."

Rachel buried her face in the hollow of his shoulder. "For how long, Jacob? Why can't Liam find and arrest him?"

He lowered his head, pressing a kiss of relief to the

top of her *kapp*. Willing his pulse to return to normal, he silently thanked God for watching over her, and that he'd left the gun in the house for her. What if she hadn't been armed? Would the kidnapper have her in the car? The thought made his blood run cold.

"*Komm*, we should go back inside," she whispered.

"Soon. First we should go to Elizabeth and David's to borrow their phone." No sooner had he said the words when he saw David hurrying toward them, armed with his rifle.

"Jacob? Rachel? Are you both okay?" David's expression was grim. "I heard the gunshot."

"We are unharmed. However, the kidnapper was here," Jacob admitted. "We need to borrow your phone to call Liam."

"Liam?" David arched a brow. "Are you sure doing so won't upset the elders?"

"I have spoken of the danger to Ezekiel Moore." It was true, but did not answer his question. Jacob was too worried about Rachel's safety to care about what the elders might think of his actions. "The kidnapper is *Englisch, ain't so*? Liam needs to know and step up his efforts to arrest this man, before he harms Rachel."

"Or you, Jacob," Rachel pointed out. She sounded steadier now, and he marveled at her courage. "Don't forget you were hit on the head last night."

"I will make the call," David said without hesitation. "Elizabeth will feel better knowing her cousin is aware of the danger."

"I'm sorry to cause Elizabeth concern while she is expecting," Rachel said softly. "Mayhap it would be better for all if I moved into the apartment above my café."

"No!" The word came out more forcefully than Jacob intended. He tried to backpedal. "I would ask you to stay within the security of the Amish community, Rachel. Better to be here than so far away."

"The sheriff's department headquarters isn't far from the café." She sighed, then added, "But I do not relish the idea of being in the apartment alone."

He wouldn't allow her to do such a thing but managed to prevent the words from tumbling from his lips. Saying that might only push Rachel closer to the idea.

"I agree with Jacob. You need to stay here among the Amish," David said. "Let me talk to Liam."

He turned to head back to the house. Elizabeth came out, carrying the phone in one hand. The married couple spoke briefly before David took the phone and made the call. Then they both came over to join them.

"Elizabeth," Jacob greeted with a nod. "I hope you are well."

"Sehr gut," she said. "*Ach*, Rachel, I'm so sorry to hear you've been targeted by evil men."

"I wish I understood what they wanted with me." Rachel sighed. "I hate knowing you might be in danger, too."

"God will keep us all safe in His care, *ain't so*?" Elizabeth smiled, but Jacob could tell she was concerned about these recent events.

"Liam is on his way." David tucked the small phone into his pocket. "He is also in agreement that staying above the café is not an option."

Rachel grimaced. "I understand. It's just frustrating to know there is danger nearby without being able to do anything about it."

"*Ach*, but you fired the rifle to scare him off," Jacob said with admiration. "That was very smart."

"I'm grateful I didn't hit anything of importance," Rachel said wryly. "I did my best to aim high, considering I've never used a gun before."

That acknowledgment made him wince. "We will have a lesson tomorrow morning, after chores."

"If I don't have to work at the Sunshine Café for Leah," Rachel agreed.

He ground his teeth together in frustration. "You must not go to the Amish Shoppe."

"I understand your concern, Jacob, but it is a place where the kidnapper would not go to look for her," David pointed out. "I believe she would be safe there."

He was about to argue, when a pair of headlights pierced the darkness. Fearing the kidnapper had returned, he quickly stepped in front of Rachel.

David did the same thing with Elizabeth. Then he said, "No need to worry. It's Liam. I recognize the license plate."

He relaxed and stepped to the side. Knowing Rachel's stubborn independence, she would want to explain what had happened herself.

Liam parked his SUV then approached the group warily. "I hear the kidnapper has returned."

"To be honest, I cannot say for certain sure, but I did see a man moving along the barn. When I shouted at him to leave, he turned and came toward me—" Her voice broke for a moment before she added, "I fired the rifle to scare him away. Seconds later, I heard a car engine. He must have parked it down the road to keep it hidden from view."

Jacob instinctively reached for her hand. He absolutely hated the way this kidnapper kept coming after her. "I didn't see him, unfortunately," he told Liam. "But I heard her shout and the gunfire."

"I only heard the gunfire, too," David added.

"No one saw the man's face or the vehicle?" Liam asked.

"No, but why haven't you found the man in the sketch or the two vehicles they've been using?" Jacob demanded.

Rachel tightened her grip on his hand as if to warn him against losing his temper. And truthfully, he was doing his best to remain calm, despite everything that had happened.

"You have a right to ask that," Liam said with a sigh. "I will tell you that we are doing our best. Garrett found a white car abandoned at the side of the highway early this afternoon, and we believe it may be the car used in the attempted kidnapping. The car was wiped down. Still, we have a forensic team going over it, searching for prints in locations that are often neglected to be wiped away, such as the seat lever and the inside of the door handle." Liam rubbed the back of his neck. "I pray we find a lead."

"A fingerprint would be helpful," Rachel agreed. "But what about the car's owner?"

Liam hesitated, as if deciding how much to tell them, then said, "We tracked down the owner. He lives in Chicago and reported the car stolen yesterday when he went out to a parking garage and found it gone." He shrugged. "Sounds like the guy is older and doesn't use his car every day. I think it must have been taken two or three days ago."

"Reported stolen yesterday, then abandoned?" Jacob stared at Liam. "It seems as if the kidnappers knew the stolen car was a liability so they quickly dumped it."

"Exactly what we believe," Liam admitted. "Which is concerning on many levels, not least of which is what sort of connections these kidnappers must have to have gotten tipped off to that information so quickly."

"Tipped off?" Rachel repeated, her brow furrowed. "I don't understand what you mean."

"Law enforcement connections," Jacob said. "That's what you're thinking, *ain't so*? That these men who are trying to kidnap Rachel are getting information from the police. Not just any police, but those back in Chicago."

"I'm afraid so." Liam's expression turned grim. "I trust my deputies. They are loyal to me and the citizens of Green Lake County. But all roads lead back to Chicago, and we have been talking to their police department about these kidnapping attempts." The sheriff turned to Rachel. "You haven't learned any more about your father, have you?"

"I learned he left the Amish Community because of some sort of danger," Rachel said softly. "Danger that has now come for me."

There was a long moment as the group digested her statement. The danger was likely linked to her past.

And it seemed likely the elders may hold the key to understanding the source of the threat.

TWELVE

"How do you know he left because of danger?" Liam demanded.

Rachel frowned. "I found a letter, well, really a short note in my mother's Bible." She glanced at Jacob, who nodded. David and Elizabeth appeared surprised at the news, too. She gestured toward the house. "*Komm*, I will show you."

"*Ach*, it's late, *ain't so*? We will head home." Elizabeth reached over to lightly squeeze her hand. "I pray you will be safe, Rachel. Jacob, too."

"Denke." Rachel managed a weak smile. "Take care of yourself, *ja*?"

"We will." David put his arm protectively around his wife. "I am thinking it's time to invest in a buggy. Especially with a baby on the way."

"Mayhap," Elizabeth agreed with a smile.

The couple headed back to their home. Rachel turned toward Liam. "We spoke with Ezekiel Moore, but he would only tell us that my father is dead, as far as the Amish are concerned. He would not speak of anything more."

Liam sighed. "I wish there was a way to convince him of the importance of this issue. He may know something to help steer us toward the source of the danger."

"And mayhap not," Jacob said. "The note says Peter Miller left because of the danger, to keep Rachel and her mother safe. I read that to mean that Peter saw the threat coming and chose to leave our community, to stop the threat from hurting his wife and daughter." He shrugged. "If so, certain sure Ezekiel and the other elders wouldn't know anything more."

Rachel hated to admit Jacob was probably right. If her father had seen the threat coming, then certain sure he would have left before others could be harmed. And the way he'd written her *mammi* a note, explaining why he'd left, lent credence to Jacob's theory.

Inside the house, she crossed over to the small chest containing her mother's things. Removing the Bible, she took out the note and handed it to Liam.

"'We'?" Liam raised a brow. "What does he mean by that?"

"I don't know," she admitted. "It's possible he had a brother with him."

"That would be something Ezekiel and the other elders would know," Liam said with a sigh. "But I have no way of making them talk to me."

"*Ach*, I tried, too." Jacob shook his head. "Even with stressing the danger, Ezekiel was not swayed. Which only reinforces our earlier thoughts. That he doesn't know anything that can help us get to the bottom of these attempts against Rachel."

Liam took a picture of the note with his phone before handing it back to her. She carefully tucked it back inside the Bible. It was the only thing she owned that belonged to her *daddi*. "Thanks, Rachel."

She nodded, doubting the note would be much help. Other than reinforcing what they'd already suspected. If her *mammi* was still alive…but no. Her mother hadn't said anything about her father in all the years since he'd been gone.

Obviously following the lead from the elders within the community.

"I don't like the idea of you and Jacob staying here alone." Liam frowned. "Especially since the kidnapper knows where to find you."

"We are not alone. Leah is here," she quickly interjected. "Sleeping now because she's not feeling well."

"Why don't all three of you come to stay with me and Shauna?" Liam offered. "For sure the killer won't find you there."

"I cannot leave the farm and the livestock," Jacob said. "But Rachel and Leah would be safer with you, Liam."

"No, I don't want to leave you alone." The mere thought of the kidnappers coming back to harm Jacob made her blood run cold. "Firing the rifle scared him off—he knows we are armed. Mayhap that will be enough to keep him away."

"It helps to know you have the rifle, but I don't think this man and his accomplice will give up so easily," Liam cautioned.

"*Ach*, I pray that they go away very soon," she said on a sigh. "Certain sure it doesn't make sense for him to stay in Green Lake while knowing you and the deputies are searching for them. If they simply left the area, the crime would go unsolved, *ain't so*?"

"If these men left town, we would continue to work the case," Liam protested. Then he grimaced. "But yes, without clues as to who is responsible for the murder and these attempts against you, there wouldn't be much of an investigation."

"Illogical for them to stay in the area," Jacob said.

"Very much so." Liam's expression turned grim. "Which is why I would prefer you stay with me and Shauna for the next few days."

Rachel shook her head, knowing Jacob could not leave the farm. "*Denke* for the gesture, but we will stay here."

"Rachel," Jacob began to protest, but she put her hand on his arm.

"We are safer together, Jacob." She held his dark gaze, her cheeks growing warm as she remembered their kiss. "I won't leave you here alone."

Jacob looked as if he wished to force her to go, and she prepared to hear more stern orders, but thankfully, he chose instead to sigh and nod. "We will stay here, but I beg you not to go to the Amish Shoppe tomorrow."

Beg? That was a first. She glanced over her shoulder at the hallway leading to the guest room where Leah was resting. She didn't want to make a promise she couldn't keep, but also felt the need to meet Jacob halfway since he'd asked, rather than demanding she not go.

"*Ja*, I will stay here." *With you*, she silently added. In truth, she would much rather stay with Jacob, even with the danger, than be safe with Liam. And not because Liam and Shauna were *Englischers*.

No, it was because of Jacob himself. She cared about him, very much.

An unsettling realization, considering this was likely the road to heartbreak.

"Denke," Jacob said, his low voice sending a shiver of awareness down her spine. *"Sehr gut."*

"If you change your mind, just give me a call." Liam grimaced, then added, "I know that means borrowing David and Elizabeth's phone. But please don't hesitate to call if you see or hear anything else suspicious." Liam pinned them with an intense gaze. "The sooner I catch these men, the better for everyone here, right?"

"*Ja*, we will," Jacob agreed. She had to give him credit for bending his rules to use the phone for nonbusiness reasons, and for calling *Englisch* law enforcement.

Two things she was certain sure Jacob had never done before in his life.

And it gave her heart a funny jolt to realize he'd done so out of concern for her.

Jacob did his best to fight back the urge to pick Rachel up and forcibly carry her to Liam's SUV. He desperately wanted her to be safe and knew staying with Liam and Shauna was the best way to do that. Yet there was no denying the familiar stubborn glint was back in Rachel's gaze.

He remembered how Elizabeth had once told him his gruff behavior had caused her to think the worst of him. His kind neighbor had thought he'd tried to harm her.

He hadn't, would never do such a thing, but her comment had made it clear he needed to change his approach. Certain sure no easy task.

Rachel herself had said the same thing.

He walked Liam outside to the SUV, glancing at the sheriff. "Liam, I know this is not my place to ask, but mayhap you could have your deputies keep an eye on this area of the highway?"

"Yes, that's the plan." Liam offered a wry smile. "However, I can't say that the occasional drive-by will provide much in the way of safety and security. My department isn't that large, and we do have other areas of crime to respond to."

Jacob understood. "I know. The Amish generally do not welcome your assistance, but I would." The truth was surprising. "I want whatever you can do to keep Rachel safe from these men."

"I want that, too," Liam assured him. He opened the driver's side door, glancing at him over his shoulder. "I agree you are safer together, Jacob. Do your best to stay close to Rachel until we have these men behind bars."

"I will." He wanted to add something about why Liam hadn't caught them already but managed to hold back. He didn't want to sound ungrateful. Certain sure Liam was doing his best with little in the way of having any solid clues to work with.

Still, it was frustrating that he'd made so little progress despite the sketch and vehicles they'd provided.

"Go inside, Jacob," Liam said. "I'll wait until you're safe before I leave."

"*Denke* for coming." Jacob turned and hurried back inside.

Through the window, he watched Liam settle behind the wheel, then drive away.

Turning to the living room, he was disappointed to

note Rachel had already retired to her room. He sat on the sofa for a moment, thinking over the past thirty minutes. Already it seemed as if hearing Rachel shout and fire the rifle to scare off the intruder happened hours ago, rather than mere minutes.

So close. If she hadn't noticed the man moving in the shadows… He lowered his head to his hands, trying not to panic. There had to be a way to keep Rachel safe for the next few days.

They'd need to stick together, starting with the early-morning chores and throughout the day. If not for the danger looming over her, he'd look forward to spending so much time with her.

Humbling to realize how different his life was now that he'd met her. That she'd come to stay with him. He lifted his head, only vaguely aware of his nagging headache, and silently thanked God for keeping her safe.

After thinking through the few tasks he'd left unfinished, he decided they could wait until morning. And surprisingly, he fell asleep the moment his head hit the pillow.

By the time dawn edged on the horizon, he awoke feeling refreshed. The scent of coffee teased his senses as he quickly changed and headed to the kitchen.

"Good morning, Jacob." Rachel's smile warmed his heart, brightening his day in a way he'd never expected. "Leah is feeling better, but I would still ask that you drive her to the Amish Shoppe."

"Of course, but you will ride with us, *ja*?" He poured himself a cup of coffee. "I would rather you didn't stay here alone."

"Certain sure that would be fine. But you should do the early-morning chores quickly, *ain't so*?"

He hesitated, trying to choose the best approach. "I would ask for your help, so we can get them finished faster."

"I can help, too," Leah offered, stepping into the kitchen. "Jacob, Rachel told me what happened last night. I'm glad you are both okay."

"Denke," he said with a nod. "We are blessed to have God watching over us, *ain't so*?"

"We are," Rachel agreed. "I have everything ready to break our fast once we've finished the chores." She dried her hands on a towel. "*Komm*, there is much to do."

Jacob had never done the chores with two women helping him. When he'd been married, Anna had done the work within the house, leaving the farm to him. It was an arrangement that worked well, especially after they'd welcomed Isaac.

But there was something to be said for working together as a team. Something he'd usually done with the rest of the Amish men when they came together to build a barn, or provide some other building needed for the community.

When they finished, he escorted them back up to the house, keeping a keen eye out for anything suspicious. Not that he expected the kidnappers to come in the bright light of day, but he preferred to be prepared for anything.

After washing up, Rachel and Leah made the morning meal. He liked Leah well enough. She was a nice girl who'd agreed to help them, but his gaze lingered on Rachel.

She was pretty, smart, hardworking and sweetly concerned about his safety when she was the actual target of the kidnappers. Yes, she was also stubborn and independent, but he could not say she was unreasonable.

At least, not most of the time.

"Jacob, would you please say grace?" Rachel looked at him expectantly once they were seated at the table.

"Loving God, we are humbled by this food You have provided for us to eat. We ask that You continue to shelter us from harm while guiding us on Your chosen path, amen."

"Amen," Leah and Rachel echoed.

"*Denke*, Jacob." Rachel smiled as she handed him fresh bread.

"Wilkom," he murmured. He knew his renewed faith in God was Rachel's doing. He silently prayed that God would give him the strength he'd need to protect her.

When they'd finished eating, the women quickly cleaned the kitchen, then donned their cloaks. Together they went out to the buggy.

He caught a couple of surprised looks as he drove to the Amish Shoppe. It was only a matter of time before Bishop Bachman asked about his intentions toward Rachel.

The idea of courting didn't fill him with the same sense of dread as it used to. But he was not convinced that Rachel would be interested in courting him.

There was no sign of the dark blue truck, and he didn't bother searching for the white car since it had already been abandoned by the kidnappers. Yet now each vehicle was suspect, and he found himself viewing each one they passed as a potential threat.

"*Ach*, there it is, Jacob," Rachel said. She smiled up at him again, and he feared he'd do anything she wanted to keep seeing it.

"Ja," he managed through a throat tight with emotion. There were several women walking to the large red barn that housed many of the individually owned shops, helping him to understand the importance of the commerce to their community. One of them was Anna's friend Margaret. He thought about Rachel's request to find out why Anna had left with their son, but wasn't sure he wanted to know.

Leah was sitting next to Rachel so he leaned forward a bit. "We will return at five o'clock to pick you up. Please do not walk home alone—it's not safe, *ain't so*?"

"Sehr gut," Leah agreed. She jumped down from the buggy before he could offer to help her. "*Denke*, I enjoyed the ride." She waved, then hurried inside with the rest of the Amish.

"Wait, there's Margaret." Without warning, Rachel jumped down from the buggy. "Margaret? Do you have a moment?"

The woman turned and smiled. "*Ja*, of course." Jacob noticed she didn't look angry with him, which was surprising. "Hello, Jacob."

"Margaret." He could feel Rachel's gaze boring into him, so he forced the question past his tight throat. "Do you remember the day Anna left with Isaac?"

"Ach, ja." Her features filled with sorrow. "The little one was sick with a fever."

Jacob frowned, thinking back. Had Anna mentioned

something about a fever? He had been working long hours watering the fields because of the drought and didn't remember a conversation about a fever.

"Wait, are you saying she used the buggy to take Isaac to the doctor?" Rachel asked.

Margaret hesitated, then nodded. "*Ja*, she was." Anna's friend glanced at him, reading the shock in his eyes. "I'm sorry, Jacob. I worried that she hadn't confided in you about where she'd gone."

"She did not, but I appreciate you telling me, Margaret." He was only slightly reassured that Anna hadn't intended to leave him.

Why hadn't Anna mentioned taking Isaac to the doctor? Then he understood that Margaret meant an *Englisch* doctor.

Not one within their community.

"*Denke*, Margaret," Rachel said. "Sorry to keep you from your work."

"It's no trouble." Margaret offered a wan smile. "Take care of yourself, Jacob. Anna would want you to, *ain't so*?"

He managed a nod, despite the guilt. Had he been so set in his ways that Anna had gone behind his back rather than talk to him directly?

Apparently so.

Rachel climbed back into the buggy. "I'm sorry if that was not what you wanted to hear, Jacob."

He shrugged. "It's the truth, which is what matters." Lifting the reins, he called, "Hiya!"

"I hope Leah manages okay," Rachel said, changing the subject.

He glanced at her. Leaving Rachel here with Leah

alone wasn't an option. And with the planting needing to be done next week, he couldn't take the day off to stay and watch over them.

Even Liam had agreed they were safer together.

Yet he also didn't want to repeat the mistakes he'd made with Anna. "I understand you wish to do your part to support the community. We will continue to pray for the danger to be over soon."

"Ja." She sighed. "I know this is for the best. I guess I miss seeing my customers each day."

"Your café has only been closed a few days." He frowned. "Not too long to make a lasting impact, *ain't so*?"

"Mayhap." She shrugged. "I guess I will focus on learning how to farm like my *daddi*."

The mention of her father made him think of Ezekiel Moore and his refusal to speak of the man. "Mayhap we should visit the Moore household again."

"Asking the same question will not result in a different answer, Jacob." Rachel hesitated, then added, "I do not wish to make Ezekiel angry."

She was probably right, but he was still frustrated by the lack of knowledge about the man. Even though he didn't really believe Ezekiel or the other elders knew what danger Peter Miller had run from, they may know something about who he left with all those years ago.

Mayhap a brother, the way Rachel believed? It seemed most likely.

A car approached from the opposite direction. He tensed, peering at it with suspicion. But of course, the tan sedan didn't stop, swerve toward them or seem interested in his horse and buggy in any way.

Thwack!

Something struck the back of the buggy with enough force to shove it forward several feet. He tightened his grip on the reins, even as a second crash from behind broke the rear axle. The buggy lurched sideways.

"Jacob," Rachel cried.

His side of the buggy slanted down. He let go of the reins as he tumbled to the ground, hitting the asphalt with his shoulder, his head bouncing off the ground. Pain ricocheted through him, and his vision blurred. Darkness threatened to overwhelm him, but he fought the urge to succumb.

He couldn't pass out! Rachel needed him!

"No, stop! Please, Lord help me!"

He pushed himself upright, Rachel's cries slicing through him like the blade of a knife. Her voice urged him to move, but his reaction time was slow as he struggled to focus through the reverberating pain. He felt as if he were swimming against the current as he freed himself from the wreck.

The rifle! Frantic, he searched for the gun he'd stored on the floor of the buggy.

Where was it? He needed the gun!

But he couldn't find it. His foot was tangled in the broken wheel. He managed to pull free, but it was too late. A man shoved Rachel into the car, her wrists bound together in front of her. He didn't recognize the man; he wasn't the guy in the sketch.

Finally, Jacob wrenched his foot free and scrambled over the broken axle. But Rachel was in the car, and the driver was already behind the wheel.

"Let her go!" he shouted.

It was no use. The car leaped forward, speeding down the highway. He caught the letters and numbers on the license plate, repeating them over and over in his mind. Then he limped back to the wrecked buggy. He found the rifle, disconnected his horse from the buggy, grabbed the long reins and wrapped them around his hands. Then he crawled up onto the animal's back with the rifle across his lap and rode directly toward town.

Liam needed to know the kidnapper had Rachel.

THIRTEEN

Rachel swallowed hard, suppressing the scream that clawed up her throat. Screaming and yelling at this man would not do any good. He'd roughly handcuffed her wrists together and warned her that he'd shoot if she gave him any trouble.

Shrinking from him, she brought her bound wrists up and subtly reached for the door handle.

"Don't bother, it's locked." He snorted in derision, as if she was an imbecile.

Of course it was locked. This wasn't the same man in the sketch. His accomplice, most likely. There had been two of them the day they'd tried to grab her from the alley behind her café.

She stared out the window for a moment, the memory of Jacob stumbling toward her embedded in her mind. He'd been pale and somewhat dazed, but his injuries could have been so much worse. She silently thanked God for protecting him. For a moment she'd feared he'd throw himself in front of the car without regard for his own life.

But he hadn't.

She struggled to remain calm. All was not lost. Jacob would seek help from Liam and mayhap even from Ezekiel Moore and Bishop Bachman. Hopefully they would find her before it was too late.

Too late for what? It was frustrating to be taken against her will for some reason she knew nothing about. She lived a plain, simple life. Keeping busy with her café, doing her part to support the Amish community.

She was no threat to this man, or anyone else for that matter. Yet, here she was, stuck in a vehicle being taken who knew where. Or why. The motive behind all this simply didn't make sense. She sneaked glances at the driver. He was younger than the man she and Jacob had helped sketch. He had dark hair and a small scar on his chin. She thought back to her customers who'd come to her café in the days before the murder.

But it was no use. This man was a stranger. Where was the other man? The killer who'd stabbed the lurker outside her café?

"Where are you taking me?"

"Shut up or I'll shove a gag in your mouth." The blunt threat made her feel sick to her stomach. She tried not to panic over imagining the worst.

The scenery outside the windows gave her the impression they were still in Green Lake County, but they could be taking her anywhere.

Mayhap even Chicago.

The possibility sent a ripple of fear down her spine. From what little she knew, Chicago was a massive city. If these men took her across state lines, she'd never be found.

Please, Lord, help me! Keep me safe in Your care!

The prayer steadied her nerves. She put her faith in God's plan, and in Jacob's strength and determination. Jacob would find Liam, and they would search for her.

After a good fifteen minutes of strained silence, the vehicle slowed. She caught a glimpse of a gravel road, and soon the black sedan was bouncing up and over the rough terrain.

Through the trees, she saw a rough-looking cabin. A mixture of apprehension and relief washed over her. On the bright side, she wasn't in Chicago. Yet reaching their destination had her wondering what fate waited for her in the dilapidated cabin.

Was this where her life would end? She didn't fear death, knowing she'd be with God, but regret stabbed deep.

Why hadn't she told Jacob how much she'd come to care for him?

How much she'd come to love him?

Rachel couldn't imagine a worse man to fall for. A man who was set in his ways, who gave orders and expected them to be followed without question.

Yet, his stern countenance had softened. He'd asked her to do things his way, rather than demanding.

And while she understood he still grieved his wife and son, she wished she'd confessed her feelings toward him.

Jacob needed to know he was loved. And deserved happiness, despite his terrible loss.

Now it might be too late for her to tell him anything.

"Get out," the driver said, shutting down the car engine. His malevolent gaze locked on hers for a long terrible moment. "And don't try anything stupid, or you'll pay the consequences."

She managed a nod of agreement, instinctively knowing she needed to cooperate long enough for Liam and Jacob to find her. He slid out from behind the wheel, then went around to her side of the car. He grabbed her arm and pulled her roughly from the vehicle. She winced as his fingers dug into her skin, but she did not cry out.

No, she would face her fate with all the bravery she could muster.

The man roughly dragged her inside the cabin. As the kidnapper pushed her into a chair, she met his gaze. "Why are you doing this?"

"I told you to shut up," he snapped. Then to her horror, he picked up several lengths of rope from the table, using them to first tie her feet to the chair, then when that was finished, he removed the handcuffs around her wrists so he could tie them to the arms of the chair in the same way, tightening them until she couldn't move.

"Please, don't do this," she begged.

"Shut up!" His shout lifted the tiny hairs on the back of her neck. His eyes flashed with fury, and for a moment she feared he'd strike her.

She shrank from him as much as she could considering her bound limbs. "Okay, I'm sorry, I didn't mean..." Her voice trailed off as he pulled a scarf from his pocket.

"No, please, I'll be quiet." Her protest fell on deaf ears. He jammed the scarf into her mouth, then wrapped the edges around her head. Tears pricked her eyes as she struggled to breathe normally. The kidnapper stood back and stared at her for a long moment before turning away.

"Stupid to go to such extreme measures," he muttered. "Better for all of us if you were dead."

Better off dead. The words swirled in her mind as the kidnapper walked across the room, then pulled out his phone. A moment later, he was talking to someone on the other end of the connection.

She strained to listen, but he spoke in a low rough voice that was difficult to understand. Who was he speaking to? The man in charge? Mayhap the man in Jacob's sketch? She wondered if this man with the dark hair had been tasked with taking her because of the sketch drawing attention to his boss. Either way, the dark-haired man's jerky movements as he paced told her he was not happy with whatever his boss was telling him.

Better off dead. She shivered and blinked back fresh tears. If she were to die here today, then she would accept God's will.

But God had also given her strength and courage, so like David going up against Goliath with nothing more than a slingshot, she would fight for as long as possible.

Pain sliced through her as she struggled against the binds. They were too tight, so much so that she feared she'd lose the circulation in her hands and feet. Casting a quick glance around the cabin, she found it sparsely furnished, with only one table, two chairs and a saggy sofa in the center of the room. There could be a bedroom or two, but she couldn't see them from where she was sitting.

Several of the windows were broken, making her think no one had lived here for quite some time. Certainly not throughout winter. There was a wood-burning stove, but the kidnapper hadn't bothered to light it for warmth.

Peering over her shoulder, she noted a couple of cabinets in the kitchen, the warped doors hanging at an awkward angle. From the little she could see through the gap, they were empty. There was nothing that could be used as a weapon.

If she was able to get free of the binds, which didn't seem likely, there could be a knife in one of the kitchen drawers. Since getting free didn't seem remotely possible, she decided not to get her hopes up about that.

Mayhap the kidnapper had planned to bring her to this abandoned cabin located in the middle of nowhere from the very beginning of this nightmare. If so, it was logical to assume they would have cleaned the place out, getting rid of anything that could be used as a weapon.

Feeling helpless and vulnerable, she watched as the agitated man paced and muttered to himself. How was it that this unstable man was tasked with bringing her here?

Nothing about this made any sense. She glanced around again, trying not to become depressed at her dire situation. How long would this man keep her here? A few hours? Until nightfall? Overnight?

There was no way to know.

All she could do was hope and pray that he didn't break down and kill her before Jacob or Liam had the opportunity to find her.

If they could even figure out where to look.

"Liam!" Jacob pressed his fingertips to his throbbing temple as he stood in the sheriff's department headquarters. Riding from the scene of the buggy crash at breakneck speed had only caused his headache to grow worse. His vision was still a bit blurry and he had to swallow hard to avoid being sick.

There was not a moment to waste. He leaned heavily on his rifle and pinned the deputy sitting behind the counter with a narrow gaze. "Call Liam right now! It's an emergency!"

For once his habit of barking orders seemed to make an impression. The deputy eyed him warily as he grabbed the phone and pushed a button. "Hey, I have an Amish guy here who wants to speak to the sheriff about an emergency. Be warned, he has a rifle with him."

"Jacob Strauss," he said between gritted teeth. "Tell him Jacob is here and Rachel has been kidnapped!"

The deputy dutifully repeated the words. Then his eyes widened. "Yessir." He lowered the phone. "Sheriff Harland is on his way."

"Sehr gut." The Pennsylvania Dutch came naturally, but the confusion in the deputy's gaze indicated he didn't understand.

It didn't matter. He moved away from the counter to lean against the closest wall, holding the gun at his side. It was that or fall, which was not an option.

All he cared about was getting Liam to search for Rachel.

"Jacob! What happened?" Liam rushed forward, his expression full of concern. "You're bleeding! Did you hit your head again? Come with me—I'll get an ice pack."

Jacob brushed off the concern. "Liam, a black car crashed into my buggy. While I was on the ground, a man grabbed Rachel. I was too slow, too clumsy to prevent her from being taken. But I have the license plate information. It's..." He frowned when his mind went completely blank. A wave of panic hit hard as he pushed to remember. What was it?

Lord, help me!

They flashed in his mind. "*Ach*, yes. Mary, Peter, Thomas, for MPT. The numbers are 388." Relieved to have something to go on, he reached out to grab Liam's arm. "Hurry, you must send the information to all your deputies. We must find her before..." He couldn't finish.

He didn't want to imagine life without Rachel. Hadn't he suffered enough loss? Anna, Isaac and now Rachel, too?

Please, God, please don't take Rachel...

"We will find her, Jacob." Liam's voice broke into his thoughts. "Let's go to my office. What can you tell me about the black car?" Liam moved to the back of the building, leaving Jacob little choice but to follow. Many eyed them warily, likely because of the rifle he carried. He hadn't wanted to leave it with the horse outside. "Two-door, four-door? Make or model?"

"I—uh, four doors." He sank into the guest chair and fought to remember. What was the make and model?

"Here. You should see a doctor, but this will help in the meantime." Liam handed him an ice pack. Jacob belatedly noticed the small refrigerator in the corner of the office.

"Denke." He propped the rifle beside him, then gratefully pressed the icy coldness to his throbbing head. Then it came to him. "Chevy. I believe the car was a Chevy. It was the same type I drove in years ago, during my *rumspringa*."

"You're doing great, Jacob." Liam's fingers flew across the keyboard for a moment, then he asked, "Wisconsin license plates? Or Illinois?"

"Ah, Wisconsin. There was a small red barn in the right upper corner, *ain't so*?"

"You have a good eye for detail." Liam's tone was encouraging. "Anything else you can remember about the car? Any bumper stickers or decals?"

Closing his eyes, he tried to envision the back end of the vehicle. But it was no use. "No," he reluctantly admitted, feeling like a failure. "I was focused on the license plate. The fact that it wasn't covered in mud was a good sign. I knew I had to memorize it."

"And you did," Liam assured him. There was a pause, then Liam frowned. "You're sure you have the letters and numbers correct?"

"*Ja*, I'm certain sure." Jacob didn't like the expression on Liam's face. "What is it? What's wrong?"

"I pulled up the DMV records, and that license plate doesn't belong to a black four-door Chevy sedan."

"It doesn't?" Jacob wanted to ask what he meant by the DMV records, but figured it was a state list. "What does that mean? I know it was a black car, with that license plate."

"I believe you, but I have a bad feeling the license plate was stolen."

"Stolen!" Jacob stared at Liam in horror. "Can't you still track the black car?"

"We will do our best." Liam reached for the phone. "Garrett? I need your help."

Jacob battled a wave of frustration laced with fear.

What if they didn't get to Rachel in time? What if the kidnapper killed her?

Although if that was the goal, why kidnap her at all? This man, and the others, could have killed her right there on the street near the buggy crash if they were so inclined. Certain sure it would have been easier than wrecking the buggy to grab her.

No, the man who'd taken her wanted her alive for some reason. Why? He wasn't sure.

"What's going on?" Garrett asked.

Liam filled in his chief deputy on the recent events. As he recited the facts, Jacob realized he'd forgotten something.

"The man in the sketch was not the one who grabbed Rachel." He looked from Garrett to Liam. "The man today was younger with dark hair, not salt-and-pepper."

"That's very interesting." Garrett glanced at Liam. "Do you think the guy in the sketch is keeping his head down for fear of being identified and arrested? Our deputies have been patrolling the county highways nonstop to find him."

"Probably," Liam agreed. "Jacob, are you sure you've never seen this man before?"

"No! I'm not sure of anything!" His sharp tone caused both men to raise their eyebrows, making him feel guilty for letting his temper slip. He understood they were trying to gather as much information as possible. "*Ach*, I'm sorry. The dark-haired man could have been the accomplice from the initial attempted kidnapping, but I cannot say for certain sure."

"Hey, I understand this is difficult." Liam's gaze was sympathetic. "Garrett, give this information to the deputies, tell them to run the plate numbers of every black Chevy sedan they come across."

"Got it." Garrett took the information from Liam and left.

"What can I do?" Jacob tossed the melted ice pack on Liam's desk. "I want to help find her."

"I need you to go home, Jacob. I want you to let the Amish elders know what happened. Maybe Ezekiel Moore will provide more information on Rachel's father. I've been searching through property records, hoping to uncover information from eighteen years ago."

Go home? No, that was not an option. He didn't believe Ezekiel Moore would bend the rules to give him additional information. "Better for me to continue riding around to help find the Chevy sedan."

"Jacob, you're hurt. You need to get some rest."

"Not that badly." He forced himself to stand, praying he wouldn't sway and fall back down. He reached for his rifle. "I will help look for her."

"You don't have a phone," Liam pointed out.

No, he didn't. But David did. "I will swing by the Amish Shoppe to borrow David's."

"Take this one." Liam rummaged in a desk drawer, pulling out a small phone. "Do you know how to use it?"

"I can dial 911." That was about as much as he knew about using such a device.

"That will work." Liam handed him the phone. "Please be careful."

"*Denke*, I will." Jacob slid the phone into his pocket without an ounce of guilt or remorse. This was an emergency situation, one in which *Englischers* were threatening Rachel.

Despite the fact he'd never personally used a phone, it was fitting to use an *Englisch* device to call for the help he'd need if he found her.

No, not if, but *when* he found her. Failure was not an option.

Jacob made his way outside to the parking lot where he'd left his horse tied to a nearby tree for shade. He'd ridden the animal hard to get here, so he took a minute to make sure the horse was unharmed, before loosening the long reins and pulling himself up on its back. Not easy to do while being injured and holding the rifle. He held the gun across his lap, while using the reins and his knees to guide the animal.

As he turned to head back to the location of the buggy crash, he considered making a detour home to get a proper saddle. But even taking that much time away from his mission was unacceptable.

Rachel had already been gone for thirty minutes. Mayhap longer.

"Hiya," he called encouragingly. Thankfully this horse was one of his best and didn't hesitate to increase his pace from a trot to a canter.

Still, the movement jarred his aching head. The ice pack had worked well, but Jacob was beginning to wonder how many hours he'd be able to search for the black Chevy before he simply blacked out from pain and exhaustion.

He silently prayed for strength and endurance as he rode to the stretch of highway where he'd last seen Rachel. God would show him the way.

Jacob recited prayers in his mind, in a way he hadn't

in the years since he'd lost Anna and Isaac, as he followed the path the black sedan had taken.

The sound of a car engine came up from behind him. He urged the horse to the side of the road, glancing back to see if it was the Chevy.

It was a police vehicle. When he belatedly recognized Liam behind the wheel, his heart quickened. Liam pulled up alongside and lowered his window.

"You found her?" Jacob asked.

"No, but I finally found a two-acre plot of land along with a small house that was once owned by Peter Miller. It changed hands a few times, so it took me a bit to track down his ownership. I need you to go home, Jacob. I will call your cell phone to let you know what I find."

"Where is this property?" Jacob asked.

"The northwest corner of the county." Liam waved a hand in the general direction. "Please, Jacob, go home before you fall off that horse."

Without waiting for an answer, Liam raised the window and drove off.

Envisioning the area in his mind, Jacob knew he could get there faster by taking a direct route through the woods and fields on horseback.

No, he wasn't heading home. He was going to find Rachel.

FOURTEEN

The kidnapper continued to pace, seemingly on the edge of a breakdown. Rachel cautiously watched him, doing her best to ignore the pain sweeping from her hands and feet from the tight bindings.

She had no way of knowing how long she'd been sitting here, waiting for—what? The man in the sketch to arrive?

Others, too?

One of the comments the kidnapper had said seemed to indicate he was getting ready to hand her off to someone else. It was a chilling thought. Not that she'd heard exactly what he'd said, but the words *you get here* had seemed to indicate he was waiting for others to arrive.

How many others? She didn't know, but even one more kidnapper would not be good. All too soon, she would understand why she'd been taken and what her future held. It took every ounce of willpower and God's strength to hold herself together, to keep from imagining the worst.

But it wasn't easy. She was human enough to fear the pain and suffering that may lead to her death.

Forcing herself to think positive, to have faith in God and Jacob, she tried to memorize the kidnapper's features. If the opportunity arose in which she was able to get away, she wanted to be able to provide a comprehensive sketch to Jacy Urban. She would be able to describe this man before her with great detail.

Yet deep down, she couldn't fathom how she might escape. At least, not without assistance. The way her arms and legs were bound, not to mention a horrible gag over her mouth, rendered her completely helpless.

She momentarily closed her eyes beneath a wave of fear and worry. It appeared as if she would continue to be at the kidnapper's mercy for the foreseeable future. As much as she believed Jacob and Liam would come to find her, she couldn't help but wonder how they would manage to search here, in this abandoned cabin located far from town.

Her only hope was that God would guide them toward her.

The kidnapper's phone rang loudly, startling her. She opened her eyes. The dark-haired man grabbed the device and snapped, "What?" He'd given up on speaking in a low voice. Again, she feared that was because she wouldn't be alive long enough to identify him.

It was frightening to watch his temper rising with every minute that passed. What if he completely lost control? From what she could tell, there wasn't much to keep him from simply killing her to be done with it. After all, she knew that was exactly what he wanted to do.

Better off dead.

"I can't hear you... The cell service out here is

terrible… You should have found a different location," the kidnapper said irritably. After another pause, he added, "Hang on."

He abruptly turned, glaring at her as if the lack of a good phone connection was her fault, before striding through the cabin and out the door.

The sound of his voice while on the phone was muffled; she couldn't make out a single thing he was saying. Still, she subtly relaxed a bit, knowing he was preoccupied. Although she knew the reprieve would be brief; it wasn't as if he'd be outside for long. So far, his conversations had been short and pointed.

While he was out of the cabin, she tried again to free herself from the bindings. Mayhap it was her imagination, but it seemed as if her left wrist was able to move, just a bit. Ignoring how the rope bit painfully into her skin, she wiggled and moved her hand to stretch the binding. Even one free hand would help.

A flash of movement caught her attention. She froze, sweeping her gaze from one window to the next.

There. On the side of the cabin opposite from where the front door was located, she saw something through the window.

Jacob? Her pulse jumped with anticipation, but the face that peered through the window was not Jacob. Or Liam.

It was a woman. An *Englisch* woman. For a long minute their gazes locked. The face in the window was identical to hers, down to the small mole on the left corner of her mouth. As if Rachel was looking into a mirror.

Well, it would be like a mirror if she was dressed as an *Englisch* woman, rather than Amish clothing.

Then the face was gone. Rachel blinked, wondering if the stress of being kidnapped was making her confused. Why would a woman who looked so much like her be at the cabin? It didn't make any sense.

Yet a minute later, the same woman tiptoed toward her, presumably coming from one of the bedrooms. Rachel couldn't tear her gaze away. She tensed, but the woman bent to whisper in her ear.

"I'm Abby. I need you to stay silent. We need to get out of here, understand?"

Rachel nodded, although dozens of questions swirled in her mind as the *Englisch* woman released the gag from her mouth, then pulled a sharp knife from her pocket to attack the ropes binding her arms and legs.

Relief at being rescued was overwhelming, but who was Abby? Why was she here? And why did she look just like Rachel?

What in the world was going on?

There was no time to ask. Tears filled her eyes as pain rippled through her hands and feet as circulation was restored. Walking wasn't easy, but she pushed herself to follow Abby through the cabin, down the hall to the bedroom.

Abby headed straight for the open window. Without saying a word, she threw one leg over the sill, then ducked to crawl out.

Rachel tried to do the same, her Amish dress hampering her progress. Abby stayed to help, sliding an arm around Rachel's waist to help her get through the opening and across the wooded area behind the cabin.

"Keep going," Abby whispered.

Rachel nodded, anxious to put distance between herself and the kidnapper. She tried to stay focused on the uneven terrain, even though her gaze continued to dart back to Abby.

"Hey, you! Stop!" A man's deep voice sent a shaft of fear through her.

"Run," Abby urged.

Rachel gritted her teeth and forced herself to move faster.

"Stop or I'll shoot!" the man cried furiously.

"Does he have a gun?" Abby asked.

The crack of gunfire answered that question. Instantly, Abby dragged Rachel down on the ground.

"Crawl," she whispered, scrambling forward across the ground on her belly.

The man with the gun would kill Abby, and mayhap Rachel, too. As Rachel crawled on her belly, again hampered by her dress, she silently prayed the woman who'd risked her life to rescue her wouldn't die today.

The sound of hooves pounding against the ground had her looking over toward the open field beyond the wooded area they were hiding within. Jacob was riding his horse toward them.

No! He'd be shot! Rachel jumped to her feet, waving her arms. "Go back, Jacob! Go back! He has a gun!"

"Rachel, get down!" Abby yanked on her arm with enough force to make Rachel stumble and fall.

She couldn't tear her gaze from Jacob, desperately fearing for his life, while in the back of her mind, she wondered how on earth Abby knew her name.

"Rachel, stay down!" Jacob clung to the back of his horse as he saw Rachel with an *Englisch* woman. He'd ridden through many fields to get here, but knew that if he hadn't caught a glimpse of the two women running, he'd never have found them.

"Jacob, go back!" Rachel pleaded from her position near a large oak tree.

"Look out!" the *Englisch* woman shouted.

When he saw the gunman, his heart squeezed painfully as the man aimed his handgun at the two women. No! Rachel! Without hesitation, Jacob brought the rifle up with both hands and fired.

"Argh!" The gunman screamed in pain as he fell backward. The gunman put his hand up to his shoulder in a way that told Jacob he'd hit his target.

Thankfully, the man rolled around on the ground, groaning and cursing. Grateful he hadn't killed him, Jacob slid from his horse, landing with a jarring thud that caused him to stumble forward. Somehow, he managed to stay on his feet, still clutching the rifle. He headed toward the injured shooter, when more gunfire echoed in the distance.

Jacob instinctively dropped to the ground, seeking cover among some brush. Who was shooting? Had additional bad guys arrived?

"Jacob?" Rachel poked her head out from behind the tree. "Are you hurt?"

"Stay back," he ordered. He wanted to check on the gunman, but he also wanted to get Rachel and the other woman to safety.

He changed direction, crawling toward Rachel's location. He was determined to get her and the other woman up on his horse, so they could ride away from here.

"Police! Throw down your weapons and place your hands on your head!"

Jacob froze, glancing toward the area where the gunman had fallen. Was this a trick?

Then Liam stepped forward, holding his weapon with two hands as he scanned the area. The shooter continued to roll on the ground, groaning in pain.

"Watch out, he has his gun," Jacob shouted in warning.

"I see it," Liam answered grimly. "Listen, I want you to drop that weapon right now!"

After a long tense moment, the shooter tossed his handgun off to the side. "I need a doctor," he moaned.

Jacob rose to his feet, stumbling toward the injured man. He had never in his life shot a human being and felt sick at the realization he had now.

Please, don't die. Please, Lord, don't let this man die.

The silent prayer reverberated through his mind as he moved forward.

"Stay back, Jacob. He may have another weapon," Liam warned. "I don't want you injured, too."

"I—shot him." He forced the words through his tight throat as he hovered nearby. "He aimed his gun at the women, saying he was going to shoot, so I fired first."

"It's okay, Jacob, I believe you. But I need you to please stay back." Liam held his gun in one hand as he leaned down to quickly search the man for another weapon.

Jacob stayed where he was, still concerned about the events that had played out before him. He glanced over to where Rachel remained behind the tree. Her gaze met his, and he tried to smile reassuringly.

"What's this, a knife?" Liam scowled as he pulled a switchblade from the guy's pocket. "Do you have any other weapons on your person?"

"No, please, I need a doctor..." The injured kidnapper's voice trailed off. Jacob swallowed hard, alarmed at the amount of blood seeping from the bullet hole in the left side of the man's chest.

"An ambulance is on the way." Liam balled up the lower portion of the man's shirt and used it as a dressing, pressing his hand down hard on the wound to staunch the bleeding. "What's your name? Why did you kidnap Rachel?"

The man groaned. "I— Tony..."

"Tony?" Liam repeated sharply. "Is that your name, Tony? Why are you here?"

"No—Tony forced me. To grab the Amish girl..." The man's eyelids fluttered closed, his face alarmingly pale.

Jacob stepped forward, desperate to learn more.

"Tony who?" Liam asked. "Come on, man, I'll make you a deal if you tell me exactly what's going on!"

"March..." The word was barely audible. Jacob stared at Liam, not sure if he'd heard it correctly.

"Tony March? Is that what you're telling me?" Liam asked, shaking the man's shoulder. "Tony March is the name of the guy who told you to kidnap Rachel?" Liam stared down at the wounded man. "Come on, stay with me! Tell me what you know."

The man's lips moved, but no sound came out. Jacob's stomach clenched painfully.

Liam dropped down, putting his ear near the man's

mouth. "Come on, tell me more. Where can I find this Tony March?"

A long silence hung in the air. Jacob knew the man had lost consciousness.

Liam confirmed his belief by reaching for his radio. "I have a perp down with a gunshot wound to the chest. Where are the EMTs?"

"They're on their way back to where you are, Sheriff," a voice answered.

Seconds later, Jacob saw a pair of emergency medical technicians burst from the wooded area around a rustic cabin, wheeling a gurney between them. He took several steps back, giving them plenty of room to maneuver.

"Hurry, he's lost a lot of blood, and is unconscious," Liam said.

The EMTs went to work, doing everything possible to save the man's life. Jacob couldn't tear his gaze away, as if he could keep the man alive by his will alone.

But it would be God's will that would decide this man's fate. Not Jacob's. He felt himself sway on his feet as the enormity of what had happened hit hard.

"Jacob? Are you okay?"

He turned so fast, he nearly fell. Rachel had crept from her hiding spot to join him.

"I'm fine." He dropped his rifle, belatedly realizing Liam would likely need it for evidence. Trying not to dwell on what he'd done, he cupped Rachel's shoulders in his hands, staring deep into her eyes. "And you, Rachel?" He raked a gaze over her, searching for signs of physical harm. When he noticed the blood around her wrists, he gasped. "What happened? How did he hurt you?"

"*Ach*, it's just from the ropes he used to bind me to the chair. I caused the bleeding when struggling to get free. I'm fine, Jacob. I knew you would come for me..." Her voice trailed off, tears filling her eyes and rolling down her cheeks.

"Please don't cry, Rachel. You're safe now." He pulled her close, wrapping his arms around her and holding on tight. She was alive, which was all that mattered. Alive and relatively unharmed.

If he had his way, he'd never let her go.

He wanted to tell her how much she meant to him. How much he cared, but the EMT's harsh voice stopped him cold.

"We're losing him."

"Get him to the hospital," Liam urged.

"He has to be stabilized in order to transport him," the EMT shot back. "Get those fluids going wide open!"

The second EMT held an IV bag up in the air, lightly squeezing it to provide the lifesaving fluids. Yet even as Jacob watched them work, he had a bad feeling it would be too little, too late.

Mayhap if he'd aimed higher, or if he'd simply tried to scare him off...

"Okay, he's a little better now. Let's get him ready to roll." The fluids must have helped enough, because the EMTs quickly buckled the injured gunman onto the gurney and began to push him back through the trees to where the ambulance waited.

"I pray he doesn't die by my hand," Jacob murmured.

Rachel lifted her head from his chest. "You only fired to protect us. I saw him aim his weapon toward us, Jacob. He'd already fired once, and threatened to shoot again. I was certain sure he would not have hesitated to follow through on his threat."

"I believe you," Liam said. He sighed, then added, "Let's go back to the squad car. I'll need both of you to start at the beginning."

Jacob would gladly sit in the vehicle to tell his story, but he'd need to bring his horse with him.

"Wait a minute, Liam." Rachel pulled out of his arms, and glanced toward the trees. "We need to find Abby."

"Abby?" Jacob belatedly remembered the *Englisch* woman who'd been with Rachel. "Is that her name?"

"Yes, and you won't believe this, but she looks very much like me." Rachel frowned. "Abby? It's safe for you to come out now."

There was no response.

"Abby?" Rachel began to run toward the woods. "Abby, where are you?"

"Are you sure Abby is real?" Liam asked in a low voice.

"*Ach*, yes, I saw her. Dressed in *Englisch* clothing, black jeans and a short-sleeved black shirt." A chill washed over him as Rachel continued searching and calling for Abby.

After a full five minutes, she returned to where he stood beside Liam. "I don't understand. Where did she go?"

"How do you know her name?" Liam asked.

"She told me her name was Abby." Rachel looked hurt. "She's the one who rescued me, Liam. She crept into the cabin and cut through the ties binding my wrists and ankles to the chair."

Jacob sent up a prayer of thanks that God had sent Abby to save Rachel.

"Why would she leave like that?" Rachel asked. "I wanted to talk to her. To see if mayhap…" Her voice trailed off, but Jacob knew what she wanted to know.

Was it possible this Abby was what Peter Miller had meant when he'd written his note to Rachel's mother? "We are safe."

Had he meant *we* as in Peter and Abby, Rachel's sister?

And if so, why would he disappear with Abby, leaving Rachel and her mother behind?

FIFTEEN

Abby was gone. Rachel insisted on looking a second time, tramping through the woods, but there was no sign of the *Englisch* woman.

The one who looked just like her.

Rachel put a shaky hand to her head, grappling with the implication. As incredible as it seemed, she felt certain Abby was her sister.

Her *twin* sister.

Envisioning Abby brought a distant memory to her mind. Laughing with another little girl as they'd picked flowers for their *mammi*, who'd smiled in appreciation of their efforts.

"Rachel?" Liam's voice broke into her thoughts. "Are you ready to give me your statement?"

Jacob stood beside her, silently supportive as she'd insisted on searching for Abby. She glanced at him. "You saw her, too, *ja*?"

"I did, and I know she is likely your sister." Jacob put a reassuring hand on her arm. "*Komm*, let's go with Liam. Certain sure Abby isn't here any longer, but mayhap Liam and his deputies will find her."

Not if Abby didn't want to be found.

As soon as the thought formed in her mind, Rachel knew it to be true. There was no doubt in her mind that Abby was somehow involved in the danger. Mayhap was in danger, too, the way Rachel had been. Abby had sneaked into the cabin to save her, but she had not seen the woman before now.

Certain sure she would have remembered seeing the mirror image of herself dressed in *Englisch* clothing if Abby had come to her café.

Turning away, she stumbled over a tree root. Instantly Jacob pulled her into his arms, steadying her. His calm strength was a balm for her frayed nerves.

First being kidnapped, tied up and gagged, then rescued by her twin sister.

And by Jacob.

She glanced up at the man who'd risked his life for her. "*Denke* for coming to find me, Jacob. I knew God would guide you to me."

"*Ach*, certain sure He did." Jacob pressed a kiss to her temple. "Which reminds me, I need to fetch my horse."

She would have liked to stay nestled in his arms, but of course Liam was waiting. Another deputy had come to pick up Jacob's rifle with gloved hands. She rested her head against Jacob's chest for a moment before pulling away. Jacob left her long enough to grab the horse's long reins, leading the animal back to where she waited. Then he took her hand, escorting her over the uneven ground to where Liam stood.

The sheriff's gaze held compassion as he stepped forward. "I know this is difficult, but the more information you can provide us, Rachel, the sooner we'll be able to find the men responsible."

She nodded, understanding he was right. The kidnapper had been shot, but certain sure he was not working alone.

"Jacob, we'll need your gun for evidence," Liam said. "We will get it back to you as soon as possible."

Jacob grimaced but nodded.

As they rounded the cabin, she drew in a quick breath upon seeing several sheriff deputy squad cars parked on the gravel drive. There were several deputies milling about. Chief Deputy Garrett Nichols was there, holding on to a man who had his hands cuffed behind his back. Oddly enough, that man was yet another stranger, not the man in the sketch.

"I'm taking this perp to jail," Garrett told Liam. "He's refusing to talk."

"Lawyer," the man growled.

"Other than saying that," Garrett amended wryly.

Liam looked frustrated but nodded. "Get him processed, fingerprinted for an ID and then let him use his phone call to obtain a lawyer. I'll be there soon."

"Got it." Garrett tugged the man toward the closest squad car. "Let's go."

"Do you know that man's name?" Jacob asked, frowning at the suspect.

"He didn't have an ID on him, but we'll run his fingerprints through the system. I have no doubt we'll get a name shortly." Liam gestured to the empty vehicle. "I would like to talk to Rachel first, Jacob, if you don't mind."

Jacob hesitated, then released her hand. "I'll wait here."

Rachel slid into the front seat of the squad car, while Liam sat behind the wheel. She started at the beginning, with the buggy crash. How she'd held on to the side of the buggy to keep herself from falling onto Jacob, only to have a man sneak up behind her, grabbing her wrist and then slipping a handcuff over it. Seconds later, both wrists were cuffed and she was placed in the black sedan.

"Was there any damage to the front end of the car?" Liam asked.

"I don't recall any, but I didn't look closely. I was concerned about Jacob falling to the ground and hitting his head."

"Understandable," Liam agreed. "Go on."

She described being gagged and bound to the chair with rope, listening to the kidnapper talk to someone about getting there soon. "He was angry and said they would be better off if I was dead."

"I'm sorry you had to go through that." Liam sighed, then added, "Although it is odd that they held you there when it would have been easier to kill you."

"Ja," she agreed. "When the kidnapper went outside to get better phone reception, the woman named Abby, who looks just like me, came to the rescue."

Liam regarded her thoughtfully. "Abby looked enough like you to be your sister."

She nodded, reaching up to touch the mole at the corner of her mouth. "Abby had this same mole, same facial features and same hair and eye color. The only difference was her clothing."

"I can't say I'm entirely surprised," Liam admitted. "All along I believed this to be a personal attack against you."

"Abby didn't attack me," she quickly protested. "I wouldn't have escaped if not for her help."

"I'm not saying she attacked you, but she must know something," Liam insisted. "Otherwise, how did she find you here at the cabin?"

Rachel stared at Liam. It was a good question, one for which she had no answer. "I—don't know."

"We'll look for her, too." Liam looked down at his small notebook for a moment. "Anything else you can remember that might help us find her, or the man in the sketch?"

She shook her head. "I wish there was more to tell you. But other than memorizing the kidnapper's face in case I needed to help with a sketch, and being rescued by Abby, there is nothing more to add."

"You did very good, Rachel," Liam assured her. "What do you remember about the shooting behind the cabin?"

She described how she and Abby had been running away when she saw Jacob. When she heard the kidnapper behind them, she warned Jacob of the danger. "I feared for his life, Liam."

"I understand. Go on."

"The man fired his gun, probably to scare us. Then he threatened to shoot us. When I saw him lift the gun, I yelled at Jacob to get back. Instead, Jacob raised his rifle and fired at the gunman." Those terrifying moments would be forever etched in her memory. And she felt awful that Jacob had been put in the position of shooting the kidnapper.

Not that she'd asked to be taken against her will. But she still wrestled with guilt over the choice Jacob had been forced to make.

Liam asked a few more questions, taking notes as she answered.

"Please know Jacob was only trying to protect us." She implored Liam to believe her. "He would never have fired at the *Englischer*, if not for him aiming his weapon toward us and threatening to shoot. Certain sure he would have killed me and Abby."

"I have no doubt Jacob saved your life, Rachel." Liam's tone was gentle. "He will not be in trouble for this incident."

"Denke," she whispered, her shoulders slumping in relief.

Liam's radio squawked and he pressed the button. "Go ahead, Garrett."

"Our guy in custody finally gave me his name, Franco Marchese. He must have realized his fingerprints are in the system."

"Marchese." Liam nodded slowly. "That's what the kidnapper was trying to say. That Tony Marchese told him to grab Rachel."

"I'm going to dig into the Marchese name," Garrett continued. "I know I've heard it before."

"You have," Liam said grimly. "They're part of an organized crime ring out of Chicago, headed up by Walter Marchese."

"What brought the Marchese family to Green Lake?" Garrett asked.

Me, Rachel thought, feeling sick to her stomach. She knew for certain sure she was the reason the Marcheses had come to their quiet, peaceful community.

What she didn't understand was what role her father played in all of this? Had he been involved with the Marchese family at some point?

It seemed likely. And worse, Rachel was convinced her twin sister knew exactly what was going on.

But Abby was gone, and looking back, Rachel realized Abby had disappeared the moment Liam had arrived. Likely, her sister had sneaked away to avoid being questioned by the local law enforcement.

She buried her face in her hands, sick at the thought she'd probably never see her sister again.

The sister she hadn't known about until a few minutes ago.

Jacob rushed forward when Rachel stepped out of Liam's police vehicle. Her features were so pale, he feared she might be suffering a relapse, the events of the kidnapping finally catching up to her. "*Ach*, Rachel, are you okay?"

"Sehr gut." She managed a lopsided smile. "It's your turn to speak with Liam, *ja*?"

"Hopefully this won't take long." He needed to get his horse home, and Rachel, too. They both needed to rest and recover after the trauma. He went back to take the horse's reins, then handed them to Rachel. "Will you hold him for me?"

"Of course." She took the reins readily enough. He hoped that tending to the animal would give her something to focus on, other than her missing twin sister.

His conversation with Liam didn't take long. He reiterated the events leading up to his shooting the gunman. Liam took notes, then nodded.

"Your story is the same as Rachel's, and I know you would not have taken such drastic actions without a good reason."

Jacob nodded. "*Denke.* I appreciate your understanding, Liam."

There was a brief hesitation before Liam asked, "Do you know anything about Walter or Tony Marchese?"

Remembering the gunman's last whispered words, he slowly shook his head. "No, but it seems as if the kidnapper mentioned Tony Marchese's name as the person who targeted Rachel, *ain't so*?"

"Yes." Liam rubbed his jaw, his expression thoughtful. "Walter Marchese is the patriarch of the Marchese family. Garrett has already pulled some preliminary information about them. Tony is one son, then there is Walter's brother, Edwardo, who also has a son named Franco. Franco is the man we currently have in custody. I'm not sure who is at the hospital, though."

The names swirled through Jacob's mind. "How does this relate to Rachel?"

"Tony is the oldest son of Walter, but there is a younger son named Paulie Marchese. The problem is that Paulie has been off the radar for years. In fact he's presumed dead." Liam met Jacob's gaze directly. "I believe Paulie Marchese and Peter Miller are the same man."

Jacob glanced out the window to where Rachel stood smoothing her hand over the horse's coat. "Rachel's father left the Marchese family years ago to start a new life here, among the Amish."

"Exactly," Liam said. "And something must have scared him off, forcing him to leave his wife and daughter behind."

Jacob turned to frown at Liam. "But he took Abby with him? Directly into danger? That doesn't make any sense."

"I don't have all the answers yet," Liam agreed. "It could be that he was with Abby when he saw the threat, while Rachel was off with her mother. Maybe taking Abby with him was the only option." He shrugged. "I'm guessing about this, as I was already gone from the Amish community by then. But Ezekiel Moore would know."

Jacob grimaced. "*Ach*, he has not been willing to speak of Peter Miller since his banishment from the community."

"Yeah." Liam lifted his hands in defeat. "We plan to keep digging into the Marchese family but, Jacob, the danger is still out there. We have two men in custody, but neither is Tony Marchese or Walter Marchese. Edwardo Marchese died ten years ago, so that's one less threat to worry about. Tony could easily find more men to send here to Green Lake, to pick up where the others failed."

Jacob winced. Liam was right. The danger was far from over.

"I need you to convince Ezekiel to reveal what he knows." Liam stared at him. "Anything that can help us find Paulie, aka Peter, or Abby, or any of the other Marchese men, is critical to ensuring Rachel's safety."

He didn't doubt Liam was right, but he wasn't sure how to convince the elders to speak of a man they considered dead.

"I will do my best," he said. "If Ezekiel will not talk, mayhap I can convince Bishop Bachman of the danger."

"Thanks, Jacob." Liam smiled wearily. "In the meantime, we will continue to look for the Marchese family members. I need to contact the FBI. I'm sure they're aware of the Marchese criminal activity."

"*Ja*, certain sure they are." Jacob reached for the door handle, then turned back to the sheriff. "Liam, who is the man in the sketch?"

"Garrett confirmed your sketch matches the mug shot of Tony Marchese. Now that we have Franco Marchese in custody, we might be able to work with him on a lighter sentence if he hands over his cousin Tony. At least, that's the plan we're going to run by the Feds."

"And if he doesn't?"

Liam sighed. "Then we'll keep searching for Tony ourselves." He hesitated, then added, "Please tell Rachel to be careful if she sees Abby again. While I'm grateful her sister helped rescue Rachel from the cabin, I can't help but think she's involved with the Marchese family business. In some way or another."

"I will." There was no doubt in Jacob's mind that Abby was part of this. Why else would she leave on her own, without so much as speaking with the police?

"Do you want me to give you a ride home?" Liam asked.

"Certain sure Rachel needs a ride." Jacob gestured to his horse. "I'll ride the horse but would ask you to stay with Rachel until I can get there."

"That's not a problem," Liam assured him. Then he smiled grimly. "Based on how you beat me here, I'm sure it won't take you long to get back."

"Sehr gut." As he climbed out of the squad car, Jacob knew it would not be easy for Rachel to accept Abby's guilt. Rachel had a kind heart and would want to believe her sister was not involved, especially after the way Abby had rescued her from the cabin.

A good deed, certain sure, but not proof of innocence.

Battling exhaustion and the throbbing pain in his head, he made his way over to where Rachel stood beside his horse.

"Liam will drive you home. I'll meet you there, *ja*?" He reached for the reins.

"But you're hurt. I can see you have a terrible headache, *ain't so*?"

"I will be fine, although I would appreciate help with the chores." He summoned the strength to get back on his horse. "See you soon."

"Ja," she whispered, stepping back toward Liam.

He didn't push the horse as much as he had earlier, although he was very much anxious to get home before Rachel and Liam. The squad car pulled into the driveway as he crossed the field toward his home.

Liam escorted Rachel all the way to the barn to meet up with him. "I still don't like you both being out here alone," Liam said.

Jacob slid from the horse, already missing the rifle that Liam's deputies had taken with them. "*Ach*, I don't like it, either. Mayhap we will need to stay at your house, but I can't leave until after I've cared for the livestock."

Liam nodded. "Okay, here's the plan. You speak with Ezekiel and then ask for the community to help watch over your farm until we have Tony Marchese in custody."

He hesitated. Asking for help was not something he would normally do. But one glance at Rachel's rope-burned and bleeding wrists had him nodding in agreement. "*Ja*, I will."

"Good. I'll see if I can get your buggy towed back here, and I'll free up a deputy to head over to keep an eye on things until you and Rachel are safe at my place. It shouldn't take long for them to finish up processing the crime scene at the cabin."

A deputy would raise alarm with the elders, but Jacob didn't care. He would take all the protection the *Englisch* law enforcement would provide.

Liam gazed around the barn. "Anything else I can do for you before I go?"

Jacob knew Liam had plenty of work to do if he was to find Tony Marchese. "No, we will be fine for a short time."

"I pray that is true," Liam said softly. "But I will have a deputy here within the hour, okay?"

"Denke," Jacob said with a nod.

Liam turned and hurried back to his squad car.

Rachel chipped in to help with the horses. He sorely missed having his rifle close by, and found himself constantly looking over his shoulder, expecting to see danger around every corner.

His stomach rumbled so loudly that Rachel glanced

at him in concern. "*Ach*, I shall make the midday meal soon, *ja*?"

"After we finish here," he agreed. He wanted to be sure things were settled well enough that the men from the community would have no trouble taking over.

"I feel terrible to have brought danger to your doorstep," Rachel murmured.

"It was not you, Rachel." He refrained from mentioning the blame rested with her father. After he finished spreading hay for his horse, he set the pitchfork aside and walked toward her. He managed a smile. "Ready to head inside?"

"Very much so." Rachel turned to leave the barn, stopping abruptly when a man emerged from a nearby stall, holding a gun in his hand.

"You're not going anywhere, Rachel. Except with me."

Jacob stared in horror at the man in his sketch, Tony Marchese. He didn't have his rifle, and the pitchfork was too far away to use, especially with Rachel standing between them.

Jacob's heart pounded as his mind swirled with possible actions. He needed to stall long enough for Liam's deputy to arrive.

Yet even then, he feared the deputy would be too late.

SIXTEEN

Rachel stared at the gunman, a strange sense of calm washing over her. She suddenly understood why the man's eyes bothered her.

They were eerily similar to her own, likely inherited from her father. Which made sense now that she understood Tony Marchese was her father's older brother.

"Why do you want me to go with you?" She lifted her chin, facing him head-on. "Certain sure I'm curious. Especially after so many failed attempts over the past few days, *ain't so*?"

Tony Marchese's lip curled. "That's my business. Mine and your father's."

Her father's? She froze as the realization hit hard. "*Ach*, you wish to use me as bait to find my father?"

"I guess you're not as dumb as you look in that getup." He waved the tip of his gun at her clothing. She pulled her gaze from the ugly weapon with an effort. "Come with me without a problem and no one gets hurt. Put up a fight?" He shrugged. "I'll kill your boyfriend back there without a second thought."

Swallowing hard, she nodded. It would not surprise

her if this man decided to kill Jacob. "*Ach*, there is no need for threats. I will come with you without causing trouble."

"Tell your boyfriend to stay back," Tony warned.

"Jacob, please do as he says and let me go." She risked a quick glance over her shoulder. Jacob's grim expression, the way his fingers were curled into fists, made her heart ache. "I will be fine in God's hands, *ain't so*?"

"Enough!" Tony barked. "Let's go!"

She forced herself to take another step toward her uncle, purposefully staying directly in front of the gun to make it difficult for him to shoot at Jacob.

He would have to kill them both to do that.

A hint of movement from behind Tony caught her eye. Most likely an accomplice waiting to tie her up again. But then she realized it wasn't a man lurking back there.

It was a woman. Abby!

Would her twin rescue her a second time? She decided to keep talking to distract Tony. "I am anxious to meet my *daddi, ain't so*? I haven't seen him for over eighteen years."

"Yeah, I'm banking on the fact that he'll come out of hiding to meet you, the daughter he left behind. Now stop wasting my time." Behind Tony, she could see Abby held something long and thin in her hands, mayhap a length of steel she'd found somewhere in the barn.

For a nanosecond their gazes caught, then Abby gave an imperceptible nod of encouragement.

"*Ach*, do you mean to tell me you plan to shoot your own brother the way Cain murdered Abel?"

"What do you care?" Tony's smile was pure evil. "He left you behind— *Oomph*."

Abby had brought the length of steel down hard on the back of Tony's head.

Marchese fell forward, dropping the gun as he hit the barn floor. Without hesitation, Jacob rushed forward. He kicked the gun out of reach, grabbed Tony's wrists and twisted them behind his back. Tony groaned, but didn't move.

"Well done." Jacob nodded at her sister. "Mayhap you could find some rope?"

"Um, sure." Abby set the length of steel aside and went back toward the tack room. Moments later, she handed Jacob some rope.

Rachel knelt beside Jacob, feeling Tony's neck for a pulse. It was there, thankfully. Despite how evil this man was, she was grateful her sister hadn't been forced to kill him. Abby didn't deserve to carry that burden with her.

"Abby, how did you find us?" Rachel asked as Jacob bound Tony's wrists together.

"I've been tracking our dear uncle Tony through Green Lake," Abby admitted. "Well, I started tracking cousin Franco, but after he was arrested at the cabin, I switched to Tony. Funny, I almost ran right into Tony when I slipped around the cabin. He was on his way to get you, until he realized the cops had beat him to it. Easy enough to follow him here. Especially since I knew he'd come after you again, Rachel."

"Have you seen our father? Is he here, too?" Rachel asked.

Abby grimaced. "No, our dad has been missing for

several months now. But I have a question for you, Rachel. Have you seen my friend? A man named Greg Sharma?"

It took Rachel a moment to place the name. "*Ach*, Abby, I'm sorry but Tony Marchese stabbed him in the abdomen in the alley behind my café. I witnessed the entire thing."

Abby closed her eyes for a moment. "I was afraid of that."

"Why was your friend Greg Sharma hanging around my café in the first place?" Rachel asked.

"He was helping me. We followed Tony and Franco to Green Lake. Once I realized you might be a target, I asked Greg to keep an eye on you so I could follow Franco." Abby sighed, her expression full of regret. "It's my fault Greg is dead."

"No, the blame rests with Tony Marchese, *ain't so*?" Rachel stepped closer to comfort her sister. "How long have you known about me? That we're sisters?"

"For several years now," Abby admitted. "My dad—er, *our* dad—told me the story of how he'd escaped his father and brother to start a new life because he wasn't interested in being a criminal. He found a haven in Green Lake, became Amish, met our mother and got married. But within six years, the Marchese family found him. Dad took me with him when he realized his father and brother had found him among the Amish."

"But why take you with him, and not me and our mother?" Rachel asked.

"Dad said you were sick and being cared for by our mother in the house, while I was out in the fields with him. He recognized the man lurking nearby and knew he was in danger. Dad slipped away with me, staying away from the house. But the man continued following us, so Dad left the area, never daring to go back for you and Mom. I'm sorry, Rachel, I'm sure this is a lot to process."

"That is what Liam thought happened," Jacob said.

She nodded, trying to take heart in the fact that her father hadn't purposefully chosen one twin over the other. "Our *mammi* died last year. I wish we could have found each other sooner. She—would have wanted to meet you, Abby."

"I'm sorry, I didn't realize our mother had passed away. If not for the danger, I could have come sooner..." Abby grimaced and shrugged. Then abruptly scowled. "Hey, what are you doing?"

Rachel turned to see Jacob holding a small phone. The sight of him using the device was surprising, since to her knowledge he'd never done so before.

"I'm calling Sheriff Harland," Jacob said. "He gave me this phone to use when Rachel was in danger. Certain sure I almost forgot about it. But now he needs to come and take Tony Marchese into custody. And he'll want to talk to you, too, Abby."

"No, I can't talk to the police." Abby lifted her hands, taking a step back. "I'm sorry, Rachel, but I need to go. Now that I know you're safe from the Marchese family, I need to find our father."

"How do you know Rachel is safe from the Marchese family?" Jacob demanded in a curt tone. "What about Walter Marchese—isn't he still a threat?"

Abby arched a brow in surprise that Jacob knew about their grandfather, Walter Marchese. "He would be except he's currently in a nursing home with Alzheimer's disease." She shrugged. "With Franco and Tony in jail and out of the picture, there's nothing to worry about. The Marchese empire will crumble and fall, the way it should have years ago."

"Then why can't you talk to the police?" Rachel pressed.

Abby hesitated. "After being forced on the run eighteen years ago, our father hid with me until I was old enough to understand. When I turned twenty-one, he began working with the FBI to take down his father and brother's criminal enterprise. Only someone tried to kill him. He managed to warn me, then disappeared, dropping off the grid. Our dad believed, and I agree with him, that there was a leak within the FBI. Someone who was secretly working for Tony Marchese. That's why there was an attempt to kill our father."

A leak within the FBI? It made sense as Liam had mentioned a fear of someone within law enforcement feeding Tony Marchese information. That was how they'd known to abandon the white car.

Still, this was a lot to comprehend. Her sister was describing a world that Rachel had no experience with. An *Englisch* world, that was not as interesting as she once believed.

In that moment, Rachel realized her place was here, among the Amish. She had no desire to go with her sister amongst the *Englisch*, but desperately wished Abby would stay here, with her.

Clearly that was not an option.

"Give me a few minutes to get out of here, before

you call the sheriff," Abby said. "Please, you owe me that much."

"Fine," Jacob agreed.

"Wait!" Rachel rushed forward as her twin turned to leave. "Why not stay and talk to Liam?" *And to me*, she silently added. "He should know about this FBI leak, *ain't so*?"

"I can't." Regret flashed in Abby's eyes. "At this point, I don't trust anyone. Not even your local sheriff. And I really need to find our father. Now that the Marchese family has been eliminated as a threat, he can come out of hiding." Abby impulsively gave Rachel a quick hug. "Take care, sis. I hope our paths cross again sometime soon."

Rachel tried to hold on to her twin, but Abby pulled away and left the barn. Rachel followed, gazing after her sister as Abby picked up a small motorcycle that was lying on the ground, straddled it and took off.

In the space of a few hours Rachel had discovered she had a twin sister, then lost her just as quickly.

"Goodbye, Abby," she whispered.

"*Ach*, I'm sorry you didn't get more time with your sister." Jacob crossed over and draped his arm across her shoulders.

"Me, too." Tears welled in her eyes but she tried to console herself in knowing that the danger was over. Tony Marchese was no longer a threat.

All she could do now was pray for Abby.

And their father.

Jacob hated seeing Rachel so upset, but of course there wasn't anything he could do to change the circumstances. Hearing the story about the Marchese family made him realize how blessed he was to have had those few years with his wife and son.

Learning his wife Anna had been seeking medical care for Isaac helped blunt the pain of losing them. He still believed he was at fault for being so preoccupied by the drought that he hadn't been there for Anna and Isaac.

Yet deep down, he understood Anna's death was the direct result of a reckless *Englisch* driver. Even if Anna had told him about the need for a doctor, he probably would have allowed her to go alone so he could try to save the crops.

It was time to let go of the past, to accept that as painful as it was, losing Anna and Isaac was part of God's plan.

Before he could dial 911 on the phone Liam had given him, a squad car pulled up the driveway. Jacob belatedly noticed a gray Jeep parked just down the road a bit.

Garrett Nichols emerged from the squad car, gesturing to the Jeep. "Do you know who owns that?"

He reluctantly left Rachel's side to approach the chief deputy. "I believe it belongs to Tony Marchese. He is currently tied up in the barn."

"He is?" Garrett's eyes widened in surprise. He broke into a jog. "Show me."

Jacob led the way inside the barn. As Garrett gaped in surprise, Jacob glanced at Rachel, who still looked dazed by everything they'd learned. "That's his gun." Jacob pointed to the weapon he'd kicked out of the way.

"You hit him on the back of the head with that?" Garrett asked, pointing to the tire iron.

"My twin sister, Abby, did," Rachel said. "She saved my life twice today. I am forever in her debt."

"Where is Abby now?" Garrett asked.

"Gone. She refused to stay," Jacob added, refusing to lie about something so important. "Don't be angry, Garrett. She left because she doesn't trust law enforcement. Something about a leak within the FBI related to the Marchese family."

"A leak within the FBI? That explains a lot. We feared someone within law enforcement was helping the Marchese family." Garrett sighed heavily but used his radio to call Liam. Tony groaned and stirred, regaining consciousness.

"Okay, we'll need your statements, but the good news is that this guy is no longer a threat." Garrett hauled Tony Marchese to his feet and began to read him his rights.

Liam arrived shortly thereafter. They all went up to the house. For the second time that day, he and Rachel provided their statements about what had transpired in the barn.

"Rachel, I know your sister doesn't trust law enforcement, but if you see her again, please assure her I'm no threat." Liam pinned her with a gaze. "I'd really like to learn more about Abby and your father."

Rachel nodded. "I will try, Liam. But I wouldn't count on me seeing her again anytime soon. She's *Englisch*, not Amish, and focused on finding our father."

"Yeah, I know. I'll pray she finds your father unharmed." Liam rose to his feet.

"Liam, is the danger really over?" Jacob asked. "Are you certain sure there are no more Marchese family members to be concerned about?"

"Franco's been talking up a storm and throwing his cousin Tony under the bus in order to get less prison time," Liam said. "Coming after Rachel was Tony's idea. Franco said Tony is in charge, and now that he's in custody, the threat has been neutralized. I verified that Walter Marchese is indeed in a nursing home with a diagnosis of Alzheimer's. If there are any other low-life criminals within the family, I'm sure they'll scatter like rats without anyone to pay for their services." He smiled grimly. "I'm sure most of the money will be used to hire defense lawyers."

"Denke," Jacob said with a nod. It was exactly what Abby had said, as well. He glanced at Rachel, who looked relieved.

He and Rachel walked Liam to the door. While he was glad the danger was over, he would miss having Rachel nearby.

"*Ach*, Jacob, *denke* for everything." Rachel slipped her arm around his waist and rested her head on his shoulder. "You have been a wonderful source of strength for me over these past few days, *ain't so*?"

A sense of panic hit hard. He wasn't ready to lose her. Not yet.

Mayhap not ever.

He turned and pulled her into his arms. "I've never prayed so much in my entire life as I did over these past few hours."

"Me, too," Rachel whispered. She gazed up at him for a long moment, then rose on her tippy-toes to kiss him.

Humbled by her kiss and her warm embrace, he cradled her close, wishing he'd never have to let her go.

Jacob wanted to tell her how much he loved her, but fear of rejection held him back. He'd loved Anna, but he knew he'd made mistakes. After breaking off from their kiss, he tried to gather his thoughts.

"Mayhap after our midday meal we can go to the café to repair your broken window." He felt awkward, but pressed on. "Tomorrow is Sunday, but next week you should be able to reopen for business, *ain't so*?"

"*Ach*, you would do that for me?" Rachel asked. She searched his gaze. "I thought you did not like the idea of my working in the café so far from the community?"

He hesitated, trying to explain. "I know you are a woman of faith, Rachel. You will not stray from the community. And I know the café is important to you, so it must be important to me, as well, *ain't so*?"

Her brow furrowed as if she was trying to understand what he meant. Jacob inwardly sighed, realizing he was doing a poor job of explaining himself. The right words did not come easily, not when this was so important to him.

Important to his future, one that would be terribly bleak without her.

"I know you are still mourning your wife and son," Rachel said softly. "But I am very grateful God brought us together when I needed you the most."

"I will always miss Anna and Isaac," he admitted. "They will hold a piece of my heart, even though I know they are in a better place. I very much agree that God brought us together for a reason. To bring me back to my faith and to protect you."

"*Ach*, that is very sweet." She cupped his cheek with her hand. "I'm so glad you've found your faith."

"Rachel, would you accept my courtship? If, of course, Bishop Bachman agrees?"

Instantly a wide smile bloomed on her face. "*Ach*, yes, Jacob! Yes, I would be happy to court you." She hugged him again, then whispered, "Certain sure Bishop Bachman will agree, as he has been telling me it is well past time for me to find a suitor. And here you are, the one man I had never dreamed of courting. I deeply care for you already, Jacob."

"*Ach*, Rachel, as I care for you." He kissed her again, feeling happy for the first time in what seemed like an eternity. When they needed to breathe, he added, "I love you, Rachel. And I want you to know I will support your decision to work in the café."

She cocked her head to gaze up at him. "I love you, too. And, Jacob, we can discuss how much time I spend at the café. Building a life together is about compromise, *ain't so*? I would never discount your feelings." She grinned. "As long as you are asking rather than barking orders," she teased.

"*Ach*, I have been trying very hard not to bark orders," he admitted with a smile. "And if I should forget, you will be quick to remind me, *ja*?"

"I certainly will." Rachel smiled and kissed his cheek. "You are a wonderful man, Jacob. But I can hear your stomach growling. Certain sure you are seeking to court me only because I can cook."

"No, Rachel." He knew she was kidding, but he looked deep into her eyes. "I wish to court you because I love you. Very much."

"*Ach*, Jacob." She wrapped her arms around his neck. "I love you, too."

Her love was a blessing, one he didn't deserve. As he kissed her again, he silently promised to do whatever it took to make Rachel happy.

Because that way, he would be happy, too.

EPILOGUE

One month later...

Rachel waved Jacob to a seat in her café. "Please sit down—we shall break our fast soon."

"Denke." Jacob had been giving her rides to and from the café each day, staying long enough to break his fast in the morning, before heading back to his farm.

With Bishop Bachman's blessing, she and Jacob had been courting ever since the Marchese men had been arrested. She missed her sister, but tried not to dwell on Abby and their father. She kept them both in her prayers, which was all she could do for them.

She cherished the morning and afternoon meals she and Jacob shared together each day. His support of her café was heartening, but she couldn't help but wonder how long he would be satisfied with her spending so much time here.

After making two plates of eggs, cranberry muffins and jam, she carried them to Jacob. She set his plate before him, then took a seat beside him.

"Shall we say grace?"

"Ja." Jacob reached for her hand. "But first, Rachel, I would like to ask if you would please marry me."

His proposal seemed to come out of the blue, but looking at his intense gaze, she silently acknowledged they had been heading to this moment for several days now.

"I love you, Rachel," he said. "And it would make me very happy if we could spend the rest of our lives together. I promise I will work hard to make sure we talk through our differences." He paused, then added, "I will not make the same mistakes I did before."

"*Ach*, Jacob, I love you, too. Of course I will marry you." She smiled through happy tears. "I would be honored to become your wife, and know this, communication works both ways. We will hold each other accountable to speak our thoughts, *ja*?"

"Sehr gut," he whispered, then drew her up and into his arms. "We have been richly blessed, *ain't so*?"

"*Ja*, Jacob. We are blessed." She reveled in his kiss, then said, "I plan to work part-time after we marry."

His eyes widened and he looked almost upset by her declaration. "No, Rachel, I don't wish for you to do anything that will not make you happy and content. I know this café is important to you. We will make it work. It's been *sehr gut* these past few weeks, *ain't so*?"

"*Ja.* Jacob, you are sweet, but cutting back my hours will be my decision, made because I want to be with you." She blushed, then added, "I will be happy to be a wife and mother someday."

Jacob searched her gaze for a long moment. "Take some time to think about it," he said. "I don't want you to regret giving up this café."

"Certain sure I will not regret spending more time with you, Jacob. On the farm, and as a family." She leaned in to kiss him again, then asked, "Have you noticed James is courting Leah?"

Now Jacob smiled. "*Ja*, I noticed. They make a nice couple, *ain't so*?"

"Indeed." She paused, then decided to confide in him. This man who would soon be her husband. "Leah mentioned she may want to cut back her hours at the Sunshine Café if things go well with James. Mayhap we can work together out of the Sunshine Café once we are both settled with our respective families."

Jacob nodded slowly. "That would be wonderful, Rachel, but again, only if such an arrangement would make you happy."

"Only if that arrangement would make both of us happy," she corrected. "That is the most important thing, Jacob."

He hugged her close, kissed her again, then stepped back. "You have made me a very happy man, Rachel. But our food is growing cold."

"I can't believe you proposed before we had a chance to eat," she teased.

"This proposal has been on my lips for a while now, and I could not wait a moment longer." He took her hand, then bowed his head. "Dear Lord, we thank You for this wonderful food You have provided for us. We ask for Your grace as we plan a future together, amen."

"Amen," Rachel echoed. She glanced around the café, knowing that while it had given her purpose, especially after her mother's passing, no brick-and-mortar building was more important than the man seated beside her.

And the future blessings God had in store for them.

* * * * *

If you enjoyed this book, don't miss these other stories from Laura Scott:

Soldier's Christmas Secrets
Guarded by the Soldier
Wyoming Mountain Escape
Hiding His Holiday Witness
Rocky Mountain Standoff
Fugitive Hunt
Hiding in Plain Sight
Amish Holiday Vendetta

Dear Reader,

I hope you've enjoyed my foray into Amish suspense! I've had fun learning about the Wisconsin Amish community located in the center of the state and am impressed by their hard work and diligence.

Deadly Amish Abduction is the third and last book within the Amish community, but never fear, I won't leave Green Lake completely behind. I'm hard at work on Abby's story, and plan to bring back some familiar faces as she searches for her father.

I adore hearing from my readers! I can be found through my website at www.laurascottbooks.com, via Facebook at www.facebook.com/LauraScottBooks, Instagram at www.instagram.com/laurascottbooks/, and Twitter at twitter.com/laurascottbooks. Also, take a moment to sign up for my monthly newsletter, to learn about my new book releases! (Like Abby's story!) All subscribers receive a free novella not available for purchase on any platform.

Until next time,
Laura Scott

COMING NEXT MONTH FROM
Love Inspired Suspense

OLYMPIC MOUNTAIN PURSUIT
Pacific Northwest K-9 Unit • by Jodie Bailey

After four years in witness protection, single mom Everly Lopez thought she was safe. But when she's targeted by an assassin, she finds herself turning to the one person she can trust: K-9 officer Jackson Dean. Will Jackson keep Everly and her daughter safe...or will they become the murderer's next victims?

AMISH BLAST INVESTIGATION
by Debby Giusti

An explosion at her bakery kills a man, leaving Amish baker Becca Klein with questions and a target on her back. Now Becca must work with the victim's estranged son, Luke Snyder, to unravel the mystery behind the attacks so they don't fall into the killer's clutches.

FUGITIVE IN HIDING
Range River Bounty Hunters • by Jenna Night

When her brother is framed for murder and goes missing, Naomi Pearson is desperate to find the truth. But someone wants her silenced—permanently. Now she's under attack, and the only man who can keep her safe is bounty hunter Connor Ryan—her ex-husband. Only, someone is after him, too...

KIDNAPPED IN THE WOODS
by Deena Alexander

Journalist Rachel Davenport is stunned when an anonymous tip leads her to a derelict cabin—and an abducted teen. Now they're on the run. With a snowstorm on the way, they'll have to trust firefighter and K-9 search-and-rescuer Pat Ryan with their lives...*and* secrets.

UNCOVERING ALASKAN SECRETS
by Elisabeth Rees

After serving a prison sentence for a crime he didn't commit, ex-cop Simon Walker flees to Alaska under a new identity to evade vigilantes. But someone's been targeting police chief Dani Pearce, whose investigation of a missing girl has made unexpected enemies. Can Simon protect Dani...or will his past put her in danger?

COLD CASE CONTRABAND
by Jaycee Bullard

When undercover investigator Jonah Drake rescues police officer Carmen Hollis from an armed assailant, it looks like a coincidence...until they discover her cold case might be the key to solving his drug trafficking investigation. Can they untangle the truth before it's too late?

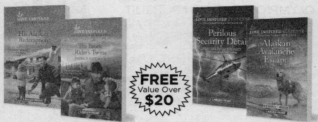

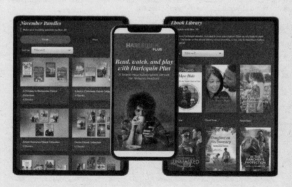